DOUBLE LONG
MURDER

ORCHARD HOLLOW 6

A.N. SAGE

OLIVERHEBERBOOKS

CONTENTS

CHAPTER 1

The walls of Bean Me Up shook violently as a storm ripped through the back office. My hair spun in wild circles over my head, the ringlets I worked hard to tame this morning coming undone. To my left, the shelf holding all our supplies vibrated from the force of the wind and I thanked the coffee gods that I had the sense to ask Joe to secure it to the wall last week. It didn't stop the coffee cups and boxes of cookies from tumbling to the ground, but at least I wouldn't get crushed to death.

Not today, Satan.

I shivered from the reference as I recalled my father. Hades wasn't exactly a demon god, but after our last encounter, I figured he didn't fare much better. Pushing all thoughts of him away, I brushed back the red mane atop my head and faced the young witch in the office.

Sweat beaded on Rory's brow as she struggled to contain the storm she created. Since I caved and allowed her to keep practicing magic in the cafe's office after hours, she had been hard at work perfecting her spellwork and potion making. For the most part, the young witch did quite well and both myself and Cilia, her coven witch aunt, were highly impressed. Then there were days like today.

My eyes drifted over the office. Or what was left of it. Everything I'd tidied after the last of our customers left was in disarray. There were loose piles of paper-work spread on the floor, the bags of beans I had loaded in from the delivery truck lay in every corner, and I could already hear Harry Houdini's hurried paws scraping on the hardwood as he rushed toward the broken cookies. Despite my best efforts, the raccoon continued to show up miraculously here and at the farmhouse. Today, though, I welcomed his thieving presence.

At least I wouldn't have to clean up cookie crumbs later. With Harry here, there would not be anything left.

"Tighten up your core," Cilia instructed, watching her niece struggle. She crossed her legs, reclining in the office chair without so much as a worry. "Breathe through the energy and direct it at the storm."

Standing between us, Rory's red cheeks puffed out. Her turquoise-colored hair fell in loose waves over her shoulders and she shifted uncomfortably, the four-inch platforms she wore today not proving to be a wise choice. I could have told her that, but Rory was a teenager and we all knew how well they listened. Still, if anyone knew a thing or two about not having a grip on witch magic, it was me.

Or at least, me back when I still thought I was a witch and not half Underworld baby.

I shook my head. Not important right now.

Before me, Rory pushed her arms out and the energy of her magic amplified. "I'm trying!"

"You're forcing it," Cilia replied calmly. Her hazel eyes flashed to me, and I swore I could see the quirk of a smile pull on her lips. The witch was enjoying this. I chuckled as Cilia casually tied up her medium-length blonde bob and shot her niece a bored glare. "Remember what we learned on Monday? Breathe into the magic. Picture it as a physical thing then blast it to smithereens!"

To my utter shock, Rory followed the instructions. She closed her eyes and concentrated, a vein pulsing on her forehead as she worked the untrained magic within her. In a flash, something shifted and her eyes snapped open, a determination forming on her features that I hadn't seen before. Rory gritted her teeth and flattened her palms in mid-air. "You messed with the wrong witch," she told the storm.

I stifled another laugh, refraining from reminding her that she was the one who created the small tornado in the first place. My gaze pulled from the practice rounds to the ruckus beside me, and I rolled my eyes, wiggling my fingers to summon my own magic. Without looking, I aimed a forefinger at the base of the shelf and let the electricity fly. It sparked as it smashed into the floor a foot away from Harry, who had polished off the last of the cookies and was beginning to tear into a fresh box. The raccoon's black, beady eyes sparkled, and he hissed, his paws scurrying to hide behind another shelf. His angry chitters ended abruptly.

I groaned.

No doubt the menace found another item to chew on back there.

Before me, Cilia continued to work on Rory, and I watched the storm slowly begin to dissipate. The pride on my friend's face as Rory contained the tornado was hard to ignore. My stomach tightened. As much as I tried not to think about it, seeing the two together reminded me so much of Gran, it made my head spin. It was decades ago when she taught me how to control magic, but it felt like yesterday. I missed her fiercely. More so lately since my wayward mother came back into the picture.

My mind reeled thinking of Mom. She was still off coffee knew where, hiding in plain sight amongst the Sisters of the River, the coven of witches we were trying to stop. So far, our attempts to fold their plan of opening the doorway to the Underworld and resurrecting my father, Hades, had proved to fail time and time again. Granted, without a vessel, dear old dad couldn't go anywhere. I tried not to dwell on the fact that he was planning to use me for that purpose and concentrated on the future instead.

We had a few weeks until the Blood Moon and the ritual the Sisters planned for. We still had time.

If only Mom had gotten somewhere.

As if on cue, my phone vibrated in my jean's pocket. I reached for it, my shoulders slumping in relief when I saw a familiar number pop up on the screen. I met Cilia's questioning gaze and held up a finger to let her know I'll be back, then slunk past Rory and her tornado. Moving swiftly, I pushed open the door leading to the alleyway out back and squeezed out, shutting it behind me with a definitive click.

The cold night air slapped at my cheeks and I instantly regretted not wearing my coat. We were officially knee-deep in winter, and Orchard Hollow was getting hit hard. The winds from the sea clashing with the cliffs did not make for fun weather.

My boots slid on the fresh-fallen snow as I hurried across the alley to hide between a concrete wall and a dumpster. Not the most fancy place to take a call, but as Gran always said, desperate times called for inappropriate shenanigans.

I wrapped a free arm around my waist and answered. "Hey, Mom," I said. "I was just thinking about you."

"That's nice, darling."

My brow scrunched. I leaned against the concrete wall, the rough texture scratching parts of exposed skin. The chill in the air penetrated my bones, but I didn't care. Something was up. "What's going on?" I asked, tension building in my abdomen.

There was a brief silence, followed by a long, exasperated sigh.

"Mom?"

"Sorry. I'm here," she replied. "I have some good news and some bad news. Which do you want first?"

Images of her getting discovered by the Sisters flashed before me, followed by the terror of what that would mean to the world. Mom couldn't be found out. Our entire realm would pay the price if Hades was allowed to cross over. I had no clue what my father planned to do once he got here, but the little I knew of him told me it wasn't anything good.

I bit my bottom lip until I tasted iron. "Give me the bad, I guess."

"You are so much like your Gran, you know that? All right, here goes. The Sisters are gearing up. They're closing ranks and everything has been hush-hush for the last few days. Whatever they have planned, they're keeping it secret. Even from other coven members."

"Do you think they know you're a double agent?"

Mother's laugh pierced the line, and I pulled the phone back before she blew out my eardrums. It took her a moment to collect herself before saying, "Piper, honestly. You are so dramatic. That ghost is rubbing off on you."

The afterlife nuisance my mother was referring to was none other than my ghost familiar and best friend —Stella Rutherford. Though I wished to argue with Mom, she wasn't wrong. Stella had a knack for being over the top, enough so that I often wondered if she was a stage performer in her previous life, even though I knew for a fact she was a very rich housewife. It seemed old habits die hard, or not at all considering Stella's current predicament, because she kept every bit of attitude she had when she was alive.

I'd never tell her this, but it was my favorite thing

about Stella. That, and the fact that she was usually pretty spot on with her comments and made for an excellent partner in crime. Especially when there were murders to be solved.

Thinking of Stella made me recall another dead woman that I hadn't thought about in some time. I pressed the phone closer to my ear and lowered my voice in case a random human happened to stumble into the alleyway and overhear me.

"Speaking of ghosts," I said to Mom. "How are you getting on with Isabella?"

A groan sounded on the other line and I froze, waiting for more bad news. Since Isabella Beaumont, resident hotel owner and dead vampire, followed my mother on her mission to infiltrate the Sisters of the River, I hadn't heard much from her. And while Stella was happy-go-lucky about not having the posh woman around, for reasons well beyond me, I worried she may have passed over in the process.

"Surprisingly," my mother said, "she is a lot to handle. Especially since she learned a few new tricks about communicating with me. I swear, that woman is mighty demanding for someone with a lot of time on her hands."

I chuckled. "She figured out she can throw things, didn't she?"

"Yes. Unfortunately." Mom let out a low whistle.

"And there is no shortage of things she's willing to break to get my attention. I'll be glad when this is all over and she's out of my hair, to be honest. I really don't know how you do this."

"It helps when you can see and hear them."

Not far from me, the back door of the cafe flew open and Cilia's head poked out. She made a motion to ask me if I was all right and I responded with a weak thumbs up. After mouthing the word "mom" and pointing to the phone, I waited until Cilia returned the smile and went back inside before regaining my focus.

"Were you able to find out anything about my powers?" I asked.

I could all but hear my mother shake her head on the line. "Not quite yet. There were some pieces here and there, but I don't think the coven knows much about Hades or his magic. They definitely don't have any information of his magic passing down through generations, though that's likely because this has never happened before."

"Look at you paving the way," I grumbled.

"Darling, I already told you before. I had no idea that your father was who he was when we made you."

I groaned. "Please don't put visuals in my head," I told her. "I guess it's too much to ask if you found out why I can hear some ghosts, but not others."

"Actually," Mom said, her voice perking up. "I have a theory on that. I think that your connection to the people who died while they were alive might have something to do with it. Like a tether of sorts. I don't know."

"It's a good theory," I whispered.

My mother clucked her tongue. "We will figure it out, honey."

"We have two weeks until the Blood Moon," I said. "Let's focus on finding the ritual place and stopping the Sisters before it's too late. That's our priority. I don't have to remind you that Hades threatened my familiar last I saw him."

My body stilled as I recalled that gruesome conversation. The Ruler of the Underworld gave me the worst ultimatum possible—give myself as a host for his being or Stella was a goner. Well, my father knew me very little if he thought I would go down without a fight. All he did was make me more determined to stop the Sisters.

And yet, determined or not, we were no closer to having a proper plan in place.

I rolled my tongue over my top teeth, the grittiness from an earlier coffee relaxing me. "Didn't you mention Joe helping?"

"I can't talk about your vampire boyfriend right now," Mom replied. "The coven called for a meeting and I'm running behind. They're in a huff. I haven't seen them this worked up since we lost Sashas Cooke. I promise to explain more later, but I have to run, honey."

With that, she hung up, leaving me alone in the alley. While I was glad that she finally called, nothing felt resolved. A part of me was hoping that I would pick up the phone and Mom would greet me with excited yelps, telling me that she cracked the case and we could save the world from Hades's vicious plans. That part was delusional, and still I couldn't help myself.

We could use the win.

A loud bang sounded inside the cafe. The walls shook and pieces of plaster fell off the outside wall as whatever the witches were doing ran amok. The back door opened, giving enough space for Harry Houdini to bolt out. His chitters echoed toward me as he darted down the alley and out of sight.

I rolled my shoulders, my lips twitching to a smile. One thing I could always count on, no matter how defeated I felt, was the surprise Orchard Hollow had in store for me. A town full of paranormals sure had a way of keeping you on your toes.

CHAPTER 2

"I recommend a mirror check before you head out. Perhaps a comb."

My jaw clicked as a scowl formed on my face. Slowly, I turned from the half-open doorway of Bean Me Up to face Stella Rutherford. Standing in the middle of the cafe, the ghost wore an unreadable expression while regarding me with a careful eye. Her long ponytail hung over one shoulder and the tennis skirt she died in swayed in the wind pouring in from outside.

As always, Stella was stunning. And unbearable.

I shut the door and stepped back inside. "I'm only going to meet Joe at the bookshop. It's not a big deal."

"Piper, please. Do not try to give me lessons on

keeping a man interested," Stella scolded. "There is simply no excuse for whatever is happening on your head right now."

A headache careened from temple to temple as I fought the urge to pummel the ghost to the ground. Not that I could actually do so without sliding through her incorporeal body, but hey, a girl could dream. Turning to leave again, I caught a glimpse of my reflection in the glass and a shiver tripped down my spine.

Ugh.

Not meeting Stella's annoying glare, I raked my fingers through the wild mane of curls and tucked the strays behind my ears. Then, spinning on my heels to face my familiar, asked, "Better?"

"Not by any definition of the word."

Sticking my tongue out, I pulled the door handle and stepped outside, leaving Stella behind. Above my head, the bell rang out as the door slammed shut and I darted down the street towards Joe's bookstore. Guilt started to gnaw at me for leaving Stella behind, but I tamped it down, refusing to give the ghost the satisfaction. Knowing her, she was already over me and on to whatever it was that kept her busy when she wasn't spending her afterlife annoying me.

Legs pumping, I half-jogged past the dark windows of neighboring businesses on Cliff Row. Joe's bookshop, Brooks Books, was a few blocks away from my cafe and I could already see the sign poking out in the distance. My mind was so preoccupied with getting out of the cold that I didn't notice the person walking in my path. The impact of a hard shoulder clipping me made me spin around. Pain shot down my arm and I yelped, rubbing the achy spot for relief.

"I'm so sorry," I said to the poor soul I tried to run down. "I wasn't paying attention and—"

My words evaporated when I saw who it was.

"Watch where you're going," Nancy Steeles hissed out.

The head witch of our local coven was out for blood, as per usual. In fact, the more I thought of it, the more I realized that I was yet to meet Nancy on a good day. And it wasn't for lack of trying. Nancy Steeles had decided ages ago that I was her enemy numero uno and there was nothing to change her mind. When she wasn't busy reminding me what a terrible witch I was—joke's on you, Nancy, because I was no witch at all—she was spreading rumors about me to anyone who would listen. The only time I had ever seen her back down was when Cilia put her in her place after she insulted me. Sometimes it paid to have friends high up in the coven.

To this day, I could not understand how Nancy and Cilia belonged to the same group of witches. The two were nothing alike, and I doubted they were friends outside their work with the coven.

I brushed away invisible lint from my jacket and faced the witch. "I didn't see you there, Nance."

"Whatever," was the response I received. It was followed by the lack of a goodbye and the sound of heels clicking on the pavement as Nancy left me in the dust.

Shaking out my hurt shoulder, I clenched my teeth and sped to my destination. By the time I reached the bookshop, I had managed to run into two more business owners that were closing up for the day. That was the thing about our little town. You couldn't walk two steps without speaking to someone. Luckily, they weren't all as icy as Nancy Steeles.

The wind pressed at my back as I maneuvered the thick door of the bookshop open and stepped inside. Around me, shelves burst at the seams under the weight of books. The smell of paper hung thick in the air and I inhaled it greedily, loving every second of being here. I had adored Brooks Books even back when it belonged to Joe's uncle, though I loved it that much more since he took over. My gaze landed on the vampire behind the counter plopped in the center of the store. Today, Joe wore a button down sweater with a white shirt that peeked out at the collar. His sleeves were rolled up to reveal a set of muscular arms and he hadn't shaved this morning, giving him a devil-may-care look.

I instinctively fixed my hair again.

"Piper! Hi!" Joe yelled out. He placed a few books into a brown paper bag and set it aside, repeating the motion for the next stack. "I'm finishing up with some online orders, but I'm nearly finished."

Teeth splitting into a smile, I closed the door behind me and flipped the open sign over, then made my way to the counter. Since we got back from our trip, it had become a nightly ritual that I meet Joe at the bookshop after locking up Bean Me Up. We would pack orders together, a new perk for the store since Joe launched the website, and chat about the day. Joe usually handled the regular books while I took care of the magical tomes saved for his paranormal customers. Since magic had to stay very well hidden, I took extra care to add in normal texts with each order so as not to draw unwanted attention. So far, it worked splendidly.

"Got any for me today?" I asked, ready to get to work.

Joe frowned. "None, I'm afraid. But if you don't mind, I haven't restocked the signed book counter yet."

I picked up a few hefty tomes from a pile beside him and carried them to a narrow side table along one wall. Taking my time to arrange the books, I moved them around until I was satisfied with the display before moving on.

"How was the day?" Joe asked when I returned. "Rory getting better?"

"At coffee? Definitely. Magic?" I grimaced. "Not exactly. Cilia is working with her, so I'm sure she'll be an expert witch in no time."

A paper-wrapped package slid toward me and I reached for the ribbon on the counter, cutting off a piece. "Actually, an interesting thing happened."

"Oh?"

"Mom called."

Joe arched a bushy brow, his lips puckering. "How is Sylvie doing?"

"You know, I'm not sure," I admitted. "She mentioned that the Sisters are up to no good but I didn't get much more. And she was acting very strange and vague when I asked her about you. It was bizarre. Why mention that she needed your help only to brush me off when I asked about it?"

Next to me, Joe stilled. His breathing slowed and I could see the discomfort clear as day as he considered my question. What was going on with both of them? It was looking like my mother and my boyfriend were keeping secrets and I didn't enjoy being out of the loop. Hastily finishing my package, I pushed it away to join the others and turned to Joe. "All right, what's going on here?" I demanded. "You're acting odd, same as Mom."

Joe raised his hands in surrender.

"Spill it," I said between clenched teeth.

"It's not what you think," he finally said. "I have no clue why Sylvie thinks I can help with the Hades situation."

I folded my arms across my chest. "But?"

"But I think it might have to do with my family."

Spit collected in my mouth and I had to tell myself to swallow. Joe had not told me much about his vampire kin, and I had not brought it up. I always assumed that he would share more when he was ready for it. Whether that was everything or nothing at all was his call to make. Following Stella's advice, I wasn't going to pry into the man's business until he invited me in. No matter how much I wanted to know everything about Joe, he was entitled to his privacy.

Except now it appeared his personal life was somehow connected to my father. I did not like where this was going.

Swallowing the hot lump in my throat, I relaxed my posture and leaned on the counter. My hip knocked a book off the tabletop and I winced as I watched Joe catch it using his vampire speed. When he returned the book back safely, I asked, "Why do you think it has anything to do with them?"

"I simply do," Joe replied with a shrug. "I know I don't talk about them and there are reasons for that, but you deserve to know who you're dating. My parents are part of the vampire coven originating in King City."

Confusion overcame me. "You don't talk to your parents because they're in a vamp coven?"

"I don't talk to them because they are the leaders of *the* coven."

Eyes widening to moons, I stared at Joe in disbelief. Somehow, I couldn't quite comprehend what he was saying. He couldn't possibly mean what I thought he'd said.

"Yes, Piper. The oldest original coven of vampires belongs to my family," he said in answer to my silent question. "The same coven that had been impossible to track after they went into hiding."

I crooked a brow his way. "Didn't they vanish because—"

"Because they brutally drained a ton of humans for blood without a care in the world?" Joe finished for me. "Correct. Which is why I want nothing to do with them. I think by now you know I am nothing like my parents."

"Of course you're not! You don't even drink real blood," I assured him. "Only the lab-made kind."

Joe nodded, his chin tucking into his wide chest. "I really hope this doesn't change things between us."

The catch in his voice made my heart ache for him. Joe was unlike any other vampire I'd met before. Sure, he had all their abilities and came with the looks most vamps were known for, but he was solid and kind. More importantly, he always put others first. Oh, and the whole no human blood thing was a huge notch on the good guy meter. For Joe to believe that I would think of him differently because of who his family was broke my heart.

I placed a hand on his arm and gave it a light squeeze. "Hello?" I said teasingly. "Daughter of a death deity over here. I am not one to judge people on the acts of their parents. Unless you have forgotten, we are quite literally in the middle of trying to stop one of mine from ending the world."

"Very true," Joe said.

He tucked a finger under my chin and tilted my head up. Inching closer, Joe closed the distance between us. His arm looped around my waist to pull me in, and I melted into his strong embrace. Joe's lips were an inch from mine when the shop's front door swung open and a throat cleared in the distance. My cheeks flamed when I realized that I forgot to lock the latch coming in. Reluctantly, I peeled myself off Joe and poked my head around him to see a slim, middle-aged man at the front of the bookshop. He had ruthlessly curly fire-red hair that clung close to his scalp, and I noticed a pair of gold-trimmed glasses tangled in the nest of it. The man coughed into his hand again as though we didn't realize he was standing there. His crooked nose poked up as he inspected a nearby shelf, waiting for Joe to acknowledge his existence.

"Leon!" my boyfriend said warmly, twisting around to face the latecomer. "I thought you weren't coming by until the morning."

The man, Leon, forced a meek smile. "It can't wait, I'm afraid," he said. "Were you able to get the text I asked after?"

What a character. The way Leon spoke, I'd assume he was plucked from a nineteen twenties movie and not someone who was younger than me. Joe must have sensed what I was thinking because he winked at me slyly while reaching for one of the book packages we had wrapped before.

Moving quickly, he cut across the shop and handed it to Leon. "Here you go. A collection of all the maps of Orchard Hollow and surrounding townships."

"Thank you greatly," Leon said.

While Joe busied himself with the customer, I continued making my way through the orders he'd collected throughout the day. As I worked, I marveled at the people who purchased from the shop. While most of them were unknown to me, I did catch quite a few names I recognized. Looking around, my chest warmed at the sight. If Joe's uncle was alive today, he would be proud of what he'd accomplished.

It was strange to think how much had changed in such a short time. If you were to tell me a year ago that this is what I'd be doing on a weekday evening, I'd have laughed in your face.

I watched Joe wave goodbye to Leon and lock the door. For good this time. His eyes narrowed on me, and he cleared the distance between us in record speed. Behind him, I could see myself in the reflection and fought a laugh. My hair was back to its unruly ways, and I was pretty sure I put my sweater on backwards this morning. Yet Joe didn't seem to care or notice. I really had it made. A thriving business, odd magic that I was finally starting to enjoy, and a boyfriend that actually liked me for me.

Take that, Stella, I thought.

How lucky was I to finally have the life I'd always wanted?

CHAPTER 3

The morning sun pierced through the curtains, blinding me temporarily with its harsh, golden light. The rays illuminated the room, casting long shadows on the walls and highlighting the dust particles floating lazily in the air. I rubbed the sleep out of my eyes, blinking several times to adjust to the sudden brightness, and stretched out, feeling my muscles loosen and my joints pop. For the first time in what felt like forever, I felt truly relaxed. Almost nearly free.

I took a deep breath, inhaling the crisp, cool air that seeped through the slightly open window. It was in these quiet times that I could think clearly, plan my day, and simply appreciate being alive. Despite the enjoyment I got from finally having a group of people in my life, there was still much to be said for quiet mornings alone.

My brain slowly woke up and I started to make a list of things I had to do today on my only day off for the week.

"Finally," Stella said from the doorway. "I thought you died."

Heart leaping into my throat, I spun in the bed to face my familiar. Stella's expression was as unenthused as always and for a second, I wondered how long she'd been standing there while I was fast asleep. I pushed the thought away because I was pretty certain the answer would give me nightmares for the rest of my life.

Pulling the covers off me, I threw my legs over the edge of the bed and sat up reluctantly. "Why must you start a perfectly wonderful day this way?"

"I'm bored," Stella announced.

I grimaced. "And that's my problem, how?"

The ghost ignored me, choosing instead to walk to my closet to inspect the clothes hanging there. She cocked her head to the side as she surveyed the selection, settling on a pair of navy jeans and an oversized sweater I inherited from Gran's wardrobe. Using a good portion of her energy, she picked up the pieces and tossed them on the bed beside me. Her eyes lit up with excitement.

Or was it mischief?

I chose to think it was the former.

"Let's go down to the beach. You could use some sun, you're looking pasty."

"It's winter," I announced.

Stella shot me a death glare and pointed to the door. "So help me, Piper. All you do is work and worry. It's your day off. Let's have some fun. When was the last time you went by the water? I bet you can't remember."

As I worked at a rebuttal, I realized how much truth her words carried. I couldn't recall when I enjoyed a beach day. Likely when Mom was here last, but that was ages ago, or at least it felt like it. What was the point of living by the water if I never took advantage of the views?

I groaned but picked up the outfit Stella chose for me. "I'll need to make a coffee to take with us."

"Don't involve me in your addictions," Stella sniped. "Meet you in the car in fifteen."

With that, the ghost vanished. My hair whipped over my face from the breeze she left behind. Checking the time, I snapped up to stand, got dressed and brushed my teeth in record time, then ran downstairs. The farmhouse was cast in a warm glow from the streaming sunrays and I slid across the hardwood floor, humming as I made my morning latte. A quick phone check to make sure I didn't miss anything important, and I was out the door.

Stella was already in the backseat of the Beetle when I stepped outside. She fixed me with a serious glare, then turned to face the window.

"You know this isn't a taxi ride, right?" I asked, climbing in.

"Believe me," Stella remarked, "no one would entrust you with passengers in this heap."

Pretending not to hear her, I put the heat on blast and pulled out of the driveway. We took the winding road around the cliffs to get to an isolated spot near the sea that Gran and I frequented when she was still alive. As I rolled the car to park, I watched Stella disappear from the backseat, only to reappear near the water. Her face, stoic and calm as she watched the waves crash to shore.

Following her lead, I grabbed my coffee, wrapped the wool scarf I brought with me extra tight, and climbed out of the car.

Despite the chilly weather, there was almost no wind where we were, the cliffs forming a protecting alcove around us. The time of year also meant that tourists weren't anywhere near, since no one was insane enough to go swimming in November. All that to say that we were completely alone.

It was miraculous.

I took a sip of coffee and looked at the horizon. Above me, seagulls squawked as they took flight, circling the beach. A ways away, I could hear the occasional whoosh of a car zooming past, but for the most part, we stood in complete silence. My brain relaxed instantly.

"This was a good idea," I admitted.

Stella scoffed. "You should listen to me more. I am full of good ideas."

"Even the time when you suggested we turn the greenhouse into a potion shop?"

Next to me, the ghost bristled. She tapped a manicured fingernail against her chin and her lips quivered into a sly grin. "In my defense, that was before I knew you were faking being a witch. And I was only looking out for your financial well-being. Sue me."

A laugh bubbled out of me as I regarded my familiar.

"I wasn't faking anything. How was I supposed to know that Mom lied about who my father was? And I'm technically still half witch."

"You're half chatty," Stella said. "Try to relax and enjoy the scenery."

Since arguing with Stella was a moot point, I lowered to the sand and watched the water with her. After a while, the rocking sound of the waves had a meditative calming effect, and I had to keep sipping coffee to stay awake. My muscles melted and I let the silence enveloping us steady my racing mind. The future held a lot of uncertainty, but sitting here with my familiar with nothing around but sea and fresh air put my heart at ease. It was the exact reminder I needed that I had people in my corner. That no matter what Hades and the Sisters of the River had planned, I didn't have to take them on alone.

A huge step forward as far as I was concerned.

"Getting out of the house was exactly what I needed."

Stella smirked in that knowing way that drove me nuts.

"Honestly, would it kill you to have some humble pie for once in your life?" I asked the ghost. "Why is it so difficult to refrain from making faces or adding snide little comments?"

"Um, who are you talking to?"

My body froze at the sound of a foreign voice behind me. I shifted on the sand, my butt suddenly frozen from the cold ground. Next to me, Stella met my gaze and swallowed hard. She jerked her head behind us as though I didn't realize that someone had seen me talking to myself a moment ago.

Slow as molasses, I leaned back and twisted around to face the other person on the beach. My mouth tightened into a thin line. *You have got to be kidding me.*

"Seriously, who were you talking to, Piper?" Nancy Steeles asked. Her head turned left and right as though we didn't both know it was only the two of us here. "Did you finally lose it?"

I shook my head and forced a smile. "Hey, Nance. Funny seeing you here."

"Because I interrupted you getting acquainted with your invisible friends?"

"Because no one comes here at this time of year," I corrected, refusing to give her insults traction.

"Yes, well," Nancy paused. "I needed space to think. I usually go for jogs on the trails but after that woman was killed there... No, thank you."

The woman she meant was none other than my familiar, who was murdered by her ex-fiancé in the depths of the forests surrounding Orchard Hollow. Even though I knew Stella had made peace with what happened and was, in fact, quite enjoying her afterlife, I still didn't like hearing her death brought up in casual conversation. Especially not by the town gossip.

I rolled my eyes skyward and let out a sigh. "I'm sure you're safe," I told Nancy. "They caught the guy who did it so you can get back to your runs."

"That's right. You were involved in it somehow, weren't you? Them finding the killer?"

I shrugged. "I helped a little."

"Becoming quite the detective, aren't you?" Nancy teased. "I suppose you need to keep yourself busy on account of not being in a coven and all. Must get lonely."

Gaze darting to Stella, I made certain she wasn't offended by the witch's previous comments, satisfied when I saw her buff her nails out with little care. My jaw tensed as I regarded Nancy again, this time without the falseness of being polite. "You know what I find lonely, Nance? That you seem to have nothing else to do than tear me down. I have a business to run, friends that care for me, and a loving boyfriend. I don't need a coven to prove my witchiness. Unlike some people."

I considered employing my magic and giving her a jolt to prove my point, but refrained. Judging by Nancy's shocked face, it wouldn't be necessary. She looked me up and down with disgust, flipped her bleached blonde hair, and turned on her heel. As I watched her storm off, sand kicking up from her ridiculously high heels, I couldn't help but chuckle.

"Wow," Stella said under her breath.. "What got into you? Not that I'm not impressed, but usually you let that witch walk all over you."

I rubbed my temples, the heat of my fingers spreading over my skin. "You know, I'm not sure. Got tired of it, I guess."

"Hmm. Perhaps you have some Hades in you, after all. It was impressive."

The idea that I was anything like my father did not sit well. I knew what Stella was trying to say, and it was high time that I stood up for myself with Nancy after dealing with her drama for decades, but still... I did not want to be compared to Hades. Did I briefly entertain the idea that my father wasn't so bad? Sure. Was I considering spending time getting to know him? Definitely. But now that I knew what he planned, there was no way I'd do any of those things again. Those were the actions of a woman who never had much in the way of parenting. Once I found out that Mom didn't simply abandon me for the heck of it, things changed. I didn't need a father figure, and I certainly didn't need one that was set on destroying everyone I cared for.

Shame on Stella for even suggesting we were similar.

My neck twisted to look into the distance. From here, I could see Nancy stomp down the beach, thinking of a way to get back at me, no doubt. Sitting there on the sand, I made a vow to let her have it if she tried. Mostly because while I didn't like how I'd handled the situation, there was truth in what I said. Nancy may not have shown it, but she was as lonely as the rest of us, more so, even.

A handful of wet sand violently slammed into the side of my head, knocking me over. I sputtered, my eyes narrowing on Stella, who held up a fistful of more sand to toss at me.

"What in the coffee gods, Stella?" I yelped.

The ghost aimed her throw. "You need to snap out of it."

"You're so dead. Again."

I jumped up and ran toward her, ready to rush right through her body. The ghost moved fast, and I ended up missing the landing and toppling over into the sand. Laughter filled the empty beach as we continued to tussle until I was too tired to stand and Stella had enough of averting my attempts. I cackled so hard, I was pretty sure Nancy could hear me wherever she ended up.

Wiping away tears, I looked at my familiar with glee. "Ready to head back?"

"That depends," Stella said.

"On what?"

She wiggled her perfect eyebrows, shot her arm out of nowhere, and threw another ball of cold, wet grains at me. Then she vanished, leaving me with a head full of sand and enough childish happiness to last a lifetime.

CHAPTER 4

"Piper! Watch out!"

My foot slammed on the brake, and the car skidded on the road. The sound of tires slicing the pavement screeched in my ears, a high-pitched wail that drowned out everything else. My fingers tightened over the steering wheel, knuckles turning white from the pressure. My chest jerked forward as we came to a sudden stop, the seat belt pulling taut against my ribcage. The force of it drove the breath from my lungs, and for a moment, all I could do was gasp for air.

I rubbed the painful spot, wincing as my fingers brushed over what was sure to become a bruise. That was going to leave a mark later. The smell of burned rubber filled the air, mixing with the faint scent of shock that clung to my skin. My heart was still pounding, adrenaline coursing through my veins, making my hands shake slightly as I loosened my grip on the wheel.

Outside the windshield, the man I nearly ran down walked at a steady pace, completely oblivious to what happened. His nose was buried in between the pages of a thick book and I recognized the title to the Orchard Hollow map guide Joe sold last night. I pulled my attention away from the book to the man behind it, recognizing him right away.

"That's Joe's customer," I told Stella, who was mid-theatrical performance in the back seat. "Leon, something or other."

The ghost patted her chest, her breath heaving with exaggerated breaths. "Leon Hunt. The cartographer."

"Wait, you know him?" I turned in the seat to face her. "And the what now?"

Stella readjusted her perfectly placed necklace and straightened out the line of her skirt. She brushed hair—that wasn't out of place—from her forehead and watched Leon cross the road, still oblivious.

"A cartographer, Piper. Someone who studies maps. And yes, I know him. Knew him," she said. "Arthur used to buy collector's maps from him to display in the study. I never understood the purpose, but it brought him joy, so what could I say?"

"Your husband was into maps, huh?"

"Not as much as that guy."

Stella nodded to Leon, who only now looked up from his book. His eyes rounded slightly when he saw me parked in the middle of the road, a look of realization dawning on his face. Quickly, he registered his mistake, his cheeks flushing a deep shade of red. With an awkward, flustered wave, his feet scrambled, nearly tripping over the edge of the sidewalk. Once safely on the pavement, he let out a nervous chuckle before proceeding to return his focus to his book.

As he walked away, I noticed a large cylindrical tube strapped securely to his back. The tube, made of worn leather with brass fittings, looked heavy and well-used, the kind of item that belonged in a museum or on one of those antique shows you see on television. It was undoubtedly filled with the maps Stella had mentioned earlier.

Strange. I hadn't realized we even had a cartographer in our town. Then again, if I was honest, I hadn't realized that was still a thing up until a moment ago. I really needed to get out more.

When Leon was well out of sight and there was no more danger of me wiping him out, I started the car and drove off. The incident had my heart racing the entire way and I couldn't wait to get home and peel off the sand-covered clothes I wore, get into a hot bath, and spend the remainder of the day being one with the couch.

"What time is Joe coming over?" Stella asked.

Shoot. I had completely forgotten we made dinner plans for the evening. I checked the vintage watch Gran left me and pushed my foot on the gas. "He said six, which means I have exactly five hours to do absolutely nothing. It's going to be marvelous."

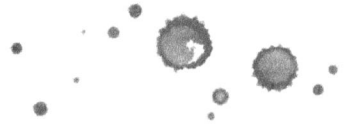

The farmhouse smelled of butter and garlic. My mouth salivated as I watched Joe work his magic at the stove, wearing my floral apron over a crisp white button down. Joe's arms flexed as he lifted the large cast-iron pan out of the oven, his muscles straining slightly under the weight. The oven door creaked softly as he shut it, then carefully checked on the status of the lamb. The meat's surface was perfectly browned, and I couldn't wait to dig in later.

"Another half hour should do it," he said.

I wiped the drool from my lips. "You are a miracle worker."

Joe chuckled and came to join me at the kitchen counter. He set the coffee cup-shaped timer and a loud ding filled the kitchen. We sat in silence for a few moments, listening to the ticking of the clock counting down.

"I can't believe he didn't even notice you," Joe said.

I told him about Leon as soon as he came by tonight, and he assured me that I was not at fault. According to Joe, the town cartographer was known for not paying attention. His mind was always on his maps and the surrounding world held little interest for the man. I couldn't blame him. There were days I would get lost in my thoughts, too.

Lifting the glass of Prosecco to my lips, I savored the sparkling drink and set it down. "He barely realized I was there, even though I almost ran him over. If it wasn't for Stella, I may not have stopped in time."

"Like I said," Joe repeated. "He lives in his own universe."

"I suppose. It did appear that he was extra out of it. That book you got for him must be super interesting."

Joe's brow creased. "I highly doubt it," he said. "Though what is interesting to me does not appeal to everyone."

"Oh?" I asked playfully. "And what might that be?"

"Well—"

His comment was interrupted by the very annoying sound of my phone ringing. Sheepishly, I reached across the counter for the cellphone, catching it right before it vibrated itself to the ground. My heart jolted at the sight of Mom's number on the screen. I flipped it around, showing it to Joe.

"Take it," he said. "I need to check on dinner, anyway."

Letting Joe handle our meal, I picked up the call and brought the phone to my ear. Heavy breathing filled the other line, and a rush of panic laced through me. Was Mom all right? Was she hurt?

I gripped the side of the kitchen counter with white knuckles. "Mom? Are you there?"

"Sorry, darling, give me a second."

A breath of relief tumbled from my lips. My lungs collapsed as I regained my composure and I peeled my clammy hand from the granite, placing it in my lap. Good. She was fine. No need to freak out.

"I'm back," my mother said breathlessly. "Had to make sure I was alone."

"Where are you?" I asked. In the kitchen, Joe's ears perked. He waved at the phone and got back to fixing dinner. "Joe says hello, by the way."

I could all but hear my mother swoon. "You tell that hunk of a man that I will see him in no time."

"Sure, Mom," I said. "Assuming you're not calling to talk to Joe?"

"I could always talk to him."

I sighed. "Seriously, what's going on? Two calls in as many days is odd, even for you. Did you find anything?"

The line went dead. I tapped the screen to see if we were still connected, putting the call on speaker. Mom's breathing filled the empty crevices of the kitchen. Suddenly, a raspy clearing of her throat shattered the silence, a sound so unexpected that both Joe and I jolted in surprise. The noise seemed to reverberate off the walls and made the entire house shake. Although my fraying nerves may have been to blame for that.

"It's possible I have a lead," she finally said.

If there was ever a moment to down champagne and celebrate, this was it. I rose off the barstool, leaning over the counter to be closer to the phone. Across from me, Joe did the same. We waited on bated breath for Mom to explain.

Finally, after an eternity of suspense, she said, "I overheard one of the Sisters mention coordinates, or at least partial ones."

"Mom!" I clapped my hands together. "That's great news! If we have the coordinates for the ritual location, we can get there early and sabotage their plans."

"It would help to know what the ritual entails," Joe added.

I grimaced. "Of course, but this is a good first step. Better than anything we've had so far." I stopped to look at the dark phone screen. "Why aren't you more excited about it?"

"Partial coordinates," my mother repeated.

A heavy weight settled on my shoulders as I deciphered what she meant. We may have had a piece of the puzzle in our hands, but it wasn't the entire thing. I wondered how much was considered partial in Mom's opinion. She could have heard anything. The excitement I felt before evaporated and was replaced by a melancholy I had become quite used to lately.

I inhaled deeply, counting to three in my head. "Is it enough for us to guess at a location?"

"I'm afraid not," Mom replied.

"Wonderful," I exhaled. "We're back to square one."

Stepping around behind me, Joe placed his hands on my tense shoulders and squeezed. "Is there anything we can do to remedy this?" he asked. "You did mention a lead."

He's right! Mom must know more or else she wouldn't have called.

"As a matter of fact," Mom said, her voice pitching,

"there is. While I didn't get the full string, I did hear Mirabel mention another tidbit that could help us. A map."

Lines creased the corners of my eyes as I narrowed them to tiny slits. "A map? What type of map?"

"I need more time to figure it out," she answered. "It sounded like a specialized one. Not any old map will do. I'm willing to bet if we have that, we might have an easier time narrowing down the location. The only problem is, I don't have the slightest idea of where to start looking."

The rock at the base of my stomach shattered. Whatever tension I held in my chest loosened up and I could finally breathe fully again. I filled my lungs, eyes catching Joe's. His lips quirked into a warm smile and I returned the gesture. Finally, an actual win.

I slid the phone closer to me on the counter. "You'll never believe it," I said to my mother. "We happen to know someone who can help out with this very specific request."

CHAPTER
5

The Inky Atlas was surprisingly easy to find, despite being on the outskirts of town and in a neighborhood I hadn't visited before. As we marched toward Leon Hunt's cartography shop, my steps faltered ever so slightly. The evening light had dimmed considerably since we left the farmhouse —our dinner on the table—and headed this way. Joe insisted we couldn't wait and, considering the emergency on our hands, I had to agree. Yet, being here now with an empty, lifeless street at our backs and the moon high above, I had my doubts.

Perhaps we should have waited until morning.

I traipsed down the narrow pathway leading to the

front door of the shop with Joe in tow. The path was lined with small, neatly trimmed hedges and an array of colorful flowers, their petals glistening with dewdrops under the soft glow of the moon. The scent of blooming jasmine filled the air, an interesting choice for an otherwise barren area.

In front of us, the red door called us further, standing out against the dark bricks of the building like a sore thumb. The paint was slightly chipped but overall; it looked like it was in great shape. Above the door, a golden sign spelled the name of the shop, each letter intricately designed and polished to a high shine, reflecting the moonlight in bright bursts of sparkle.

On either side of the door were two large bay windows, each adorned with a carefully curated display of antique maps and other ancient collectibles. The glass panes were slightly foggy, making the place seem more mysterious than it was. In one window, a beautifully detailed map of the world from the 17th century was prominently featured, surrounded by brass compasses, aged parchment scrolls, and an old magnifying glass. In the other window, there was a collection of nautical charts, globes of various sizes, and a sextant, all arranged meticulously by someone obsessed with old things.

The setup was not what I expected. I glossed my

eyes across the brick two-story building, taking it all in. People must buy maps more than I thought because this place looked expensive.

I peered into one of the dark windows, searching for some sign of life within.

"Are you sure he'll be here?" I asked Joe.

He followed my gaze, nodding. "He lives upstairs," Joe clarified. "If he's not in the shop, he'll come down."

"You know him well."

Joe shrugged. "Not particularly. He'd been in the shop a few times and I've delivered books to him here before. Leon keeps to himself for the most part, but he's a nice enough guy."

Not wasting more time, he walked up to the front door and gave it a nice, loud knock. When there was no answer on the other side, he tried again. Not giving up, Joe stood back several steps and looked up the building to the windows on the second floor. All of which were also equally dark as the shop's.

"Could he be out?" I asked.

"Possibly. Let's check around the back in case he's in the yard." He pointed to the side of the building and the shadowy passage between two large ferns. "This way."

As we slid in between the planters, my magic surged to the surface. Normally I'd coax it back in, but considering the low light and the gnawing feeling in my chest, I used the blue sparks to guide our way. Overstepping Joe, I led the way with my hands stretched outward. Each illuminated step felt like a mistake. We should not be bothering Leon this late in the night.

Sure, we had good reason to do so, but the cartographer was human, at least, as far as we knew. To him, us being here was nothing more than a nuisance. He did not know his knowledge could very well save the world tonight.

We squeezed through the opening, our feet padding softly on the ground. As we emerged on the other side, my lungs filled with air, the tightness of the space between the buildings dissipating. My eyes grew large as orbs. I wasn't sure what I was expecting, but the oasis before me wasn't it.

The same ferns we saw in the front decorated an entire wall of the building's backyard. Leaning against a wood-slatted wall was a wide outdoor lounger with two tables on either side of it. At its head, antique lanterns hung at random heights which, when illuminated, must have created an ethereal atmosphere. Across from the lounge was a stone firepit with two pokers leaning on the edge. In the far corner of the yard was a small shed that had its own charm, with white painted shutters and a rounded door belonging to an Elvish village.

I looked at Joe over my shoulder. "Quite the yard."

"Leon has his tastes," Joe replied. "Come on, the door's this way."

He led us past another set of large ferns toward a hidden staircase I hadn't noticed before. At the top of the landing was a frosted glass door with an intricate pattern etched into it and a massive bronze bell to the right. Motioning for me to come closer, Joe raised his hand to ring the bell, then stopped. His eyes widened and concern clawed its way across his features.

I tried to see what he was looking at, but all I saw was more darkness inside.

"What's wrong?" I asked, rising on my tiptoes to glance over Joe's wide shoulders.

Not answering, he pointed to the door. I swallowed a thick lump when I realized it was slightly ajar. I side-glanced at Joe. "Is that normal?"

Shaking his head no, he stepped around me and quietly pushed the back door open. It creaked lightly, the sound echoing through the yard and making my heart pound against my ribcage.

Light on his feet, Joe slipped into the darkness of the map shop, leaving me to contemplate my next move. Without a second thought, I followed him in. It took a second for my eyes to adjust to the pitch black and I stood still until I was sure I wouldn't knock into something while maneuvering through the space. From this part of the building, I could see the front shop quite well. The display window directly in front of us helped light some of the shelves and tables and it didn't take me long to make out the layout of the place. One thing stuck out though—for a map shop, I didn't notice too many around. Perhaps Leon stored them somewhere else after closing.

Joe, on the other hand, rolled through the shop like it was broad daylight. *Must be nice to have vamp vision.*

I took a tentative step forward. As I did, my magic hit me like a brick, blindsiding me. Blue sparks flew from my skin and lit up the surrounding area in their eerie glow. My head felt like it was on fire and there was a strange pull in my belly, beckoning me deeper into the building. It was like there was a string being pulled tight between me and whatever was in there. I knew this feeling well by now.

Shivering, I reached for Joe, pulling him backward. "Oh, no."

He paused to look me over. "What is it?"

"You said Leon is human, right?"

"Of course," Joe replied. "As far as I know."

He sounded a lot less sure now that I posed the

question. My belly rumbled, and tingles raked down my spine. Rolling my shoulders, I pointed toward the spiral staircase to the right of us leading to the second floor.

"There's a talisman in this building. I can feel it."

It had been some time since I'd sensed the pull of magic coming from a family talisman. While not all paranormals carried one, or even owned one for that matter, the lucky ones to get their hands on a talisman often kept it out of sight. No one would dare show off the source of generations' worth of family power. My heart ached for the brooch Gran bestowed on me before she died, the same one that shattered during one of my escapades of trying to catch a killer. It was strange how I almost never thought about it anymore. Partly because I doubted it did anything for my new brand of Hades magic, but mostly because I now knew that all my energy came from within, not from anywhere else. It was probably why I was able to tap into other paranormals' talisman powers when nobody else had been known to do that. Stella said it was thanks to me having the magic of an actual deity coursing through my veins that it made me more powerful.

I chalked it up to being lucky.

"Are you sure?"

"Definitely. Upstairs."

Fingers lacing through mine, Joe gave me a curt nod, and we took to the stairs. The twisting ascent made my head spin and by the time we reached the second floor, I was fighting dizziness, like I had climbed a mountain. Though I was certain the magic that was now pummeling me at cannonball speeds had a lot to do with it.

This level of the building was better lit thanks to the row of windows taking up the entire far wall across from us. From where we stood on the landing, I could see a leather sectional, a large television, and two tall bookcases full of weathered tomes. If I had to guess, I'd wager they were all about maps.

I looked to our left, where a long hallway led to two other doors. "I feel weird. What if Leon's home?"

"If he was, he would have come down when I knocked," Joe said. "I don't like this. It feels wrong."

I had to agree. Against my better judgment, I pulled Joe behind me and made a beeline for the hallway. The first door we checked led to a small bathroom with enough space for a stand-up shower and other necessities. There was nothing out of place here and the pull I felt before lessened when we stepped inside. The talisman wasn't here. And from the looks of it, it was beginning to appear that Leon was nowhere to be found, either.

Anxiety gripped my bones as I walked on unsure

legs toward the second door. As we opened it, guilt immediately settled in my body and after a quick scan of Leon's bedroom, I shut the door behind me and turned around. To the far end of the hallway stood one final room. Its door was the same dark mahogany as the other two, but something about it made me want to go inside. I exchanged twin looks of worry with Joe and followed my gut.

Hand trembling, I reached for the doorknob, twisting the golden metal and pushing my way in. Behind me, Joe's body filled the doorway as we inspected the space we stood in. Two of the walls in the room were stacked with floor to ceiling bookcases filled to the brim with thick spines and worn out leather. Between them, facing a large window, stood an old oak desk. There were a few maps unrolled on the desk and a deep basket, holding several more on the floor beside it.

I looked around, realizing what was bothering me about this place. For a cartographer, other than the few maps on the table, there weren't many others around, same as the downstairs level. I scratched my head, my finger on the pulse of an idea, but not quite reaching it. Behind me, Joe cleared his throat and nudged me back to the present moment.

In the center of the desk, with its back turned to us, was a massive armchair. The back of it stood so high I couldn't see over, but as the moonlight shone in from the window, I glimpsed a set of reddish curls peeking out of the top.

I elbowed Joe in the side, pointing to the chair.

"Leon?" Joe asked.

No answer.

"Is he...?"

Joe's words fell away into silence. Inside, my lungs fought for air as the realization of what we'd discovered hit me. With careful steps, I cleared the space between the door and the armchair, my stomach turning as I walked to look around it.

"No," I whispered.

Sitting slumped over in the armchair was Leon Hunt. His eyes were closed and I could tell his chest wasn't moving, lips blue and without any life at all. My shoulders collapsed, spine curving slightly to match Leon's posture. Beside me, Joe gasped and pulled me away, but I fought him off. My hands sparked with magic and I followed its incessant pull to Leon's right hand and the antiquated gold pen he clutched in his cold, dead fingers.

"Is that the talisman?" Joe asked.

I nodded. "What kind of paranormal was he?"

"I don't know," Joe replied. "Not a vampire. I'd smell the blood if he was. Maybe a warlock?"

Wincing, I turned away from the body. Whatever

Leon Hunt was, it didn't matter anymore, did it? At my back, the talisman called for me, aching to be used. I shut myself off to its energy, folding my arms across my chest while Joe called the police. A lot of good family magic did Leon. He died before he had the chance to use any of it.

CHAPTER 6

I f I had a penny for every time I found myself at the police station, I'd retire. Joe and I filed into the crammed interview room at the back of the station and settled into two of the least comfortable chairs the world had ever known. Seriously, these could be used as torture devices if one ever required them.

Around us, the bland interior of the room added to the already dreary mood overtaking me and I tried not to think about Leon Hunt, focusing instead on the peeling white paint on the concrete walls. The smell of steel and bleach permeated my nostrils with every breath.

Lovely.

Down the corridor, I could hear Sheriff Romero's grumbles as he ordered the officers on shift tonight around. I caught only bits of the conversation, but I knew what the sheriff was upset about without even trying. Another death in Orchard Hollow. It was uncanny how many there were recently. Truly impossible by all rational standards.

And yet it wasn't. Not with the daughter of Hades around. Death had magnetized itself to me, so it was fair to assume that it would follow wherever I went.

"How much are we letting on?" Joe asked.

What he meant to ask was whether we were going to tell the sheriff about the magic I sensed or that Leon was likely a paranormal, though we were yet to figure out which type. Unlike most other humans in our town, Sheriff Romero was in on Orchard Hollow's deep, dark secret about the things that go bump in the night. It was why he was stationed here in the first place. Yet despite knowing the truth, he was yet to make his peace with it. At least, that was the impression I got after my recent dealings with the man.

The sheriff knew all about magic, but he preferred to keep his nose out of it. Which was usually where I came into the picture. A little trade off after I helped solve several cases in the past.

Needless to say, I got the crummy end of that stick.

"I don't care what time of night it is, Randolf!" the sheriff shouted. "Get it done!"

Loud, angry steps neared us. I sat up straight in the chair as I heard Romero storm closer to our room. Behind him, muffled conversation and panicked voices carried through the station as the rest of the force picked up on his manic energy.

"Is it me, or is he worse this time?" I asked Joe.

My boyfriend raised one thick brow. "I can't say I would know the difference."

Of course he wouldn't. I was the only one lucky enough to see the sheriff on a regular basis.

The steps got nearer still and a moment later, Sheriff Romero's boots were stomping into the room. His brows were so closely knit together, they formed one large caterpillar above his eyes. His frown deepened when his heated gaze landed on Joe and me. "Miss Addison. Mister Brooks," the sheriff grumbled. "I would say I'm surprised to see you here, but I think we all know that would be a lie."

"Look, Sheriff—"

Romero raised a finger in the air to cut me off. Scowling, he removed his wide-brimmed hat and placed it on the table between us. I was relieved to see his signature thick mustache back and stifled a giggle when the sheriff curled it at the edges instinctively.

"Let's cut the niceties," Romero said as he took a seat opposite us. "Tell me what happened."

Niceties? The sheriff and I had very different definitions of the word because I was yet to feel nice and cozy in this place.

I tried to keep my eyes ahead and not get distracted by Joe next to me. Despite my better effort, I could feel the warmth of his skin on my arm and it distracted me to no small bounds. Between the two of us, Joe was much better equipped to deal with the police due to his history of being a big shot lawyer in the city in a past life. And yet I could tell he was nervous, too.

Sheriff Romero had a tendency to bring that out in people.

I reached under the desk and placed my hand on Joe's thigh, then turned my focus back to the sheriff. "I'm sure the officers on scene filled you in, Sheriff," I said. "Leon Hunt was dead when we arrived and I'm not certain how long he'd been that way."

"At least two hours," Joe corrected.

I glared at my boyfriend in sheer surprise.

"Vampire scent," he explained. "His blood was...less fresh."

Ew gross. I worked hard to keep my dinner down, narrowing my sights on the sheriff and not my vampire boyfriend, who apparently had plenty of time to smell

Leon's corpse. "Well, there you have it. Couldn't have been us."

"I never implied otherwise, Miss Addison," Romero said. His hands shot up in defense, and he quickly lowered them back down. "What I'd like to know is why you were there. At the scene of a murder. Once again."

My chest fought to contain the runner's heart galloping in its cage. A bead of sweat rolled down my neck and fell beneath the confines of the cowl neck sweater I wore. Spine rigid, I fiddled with a chipped nail while Romero stared me down. I should lie. I should spin a tale like I always do to keep him safe and away from the dark truth of Hades and his coven. And yet I no longer wanted to do that. Somewhere along the way, I stopped wanting to keep the sheriff in the dark. We both wished for nothing but safety for the town, the same but different.

I pulled my hand away from Joe's thigh.

I surrendered.

"Okay, Sheriff," I said. "What I'm about to say may seem extreme, but I beg you to keep an open mind."

"Miss Addison. I know all about magic and para-normals. Nothing could shock me."

I scoffed. "Want to bet?"

Then I took a deep breath and told him everything.

By the time I was done speaking, the frustration on Romero's face melted away, making room for an entire new arsenal of emotions. As I watched the man go from horrified, to surprised, to intrigued, back to horrified again. All fair responses to someone telling you that the God of Death plans to take over the Earth any day unless a clumsy witch and her paranormal friends can find a way to stop him.

The one thing I never saw Romero do was question what I said. He didn't crook a brow or look at me like I may have been exaggerating or lying. It was nice to see that after all this time of somewhat working together to rid Orchard Hollow of bad people, we had mutual respect between us.

Finally, I kind of sort of belonged.

"And that's why we were at Leon's," I finished. "To find the map."

Before me, Sheriff Romero twirled his mustache again and his gaze darted from me to Joe. He cleared his throat, his hands cupped together. "Interesting story," he said.

"It's the truth."

The sheriff tightened his lips. "I never said it wasn't. Only that it was interesting." He pulled back his chair, the metal legs scraping against the floor and making my teeth itch. "I suppose you'll want to get out of here."

Wait, what?

I stared at him, baffled.

"That's it?" I asked. "No lecture, no telling me to stay out of the investigation. Not even a "leave it to the law, Miss Addison, before the law comes after you." Really?"

An unexpected chuckle tumbled from the sheriff's mouth. "Is that what I sound like?" He sighed, leaning on the table. When he looked up at me from behind the brim of his hat, I stopped breathing. "I have seen enough in this town to know when to get involved and when to look the other way," the sheriff said. "While I'd love to be able to tell you that me and my guys have this handled, I think we both know that would be a far stretch from the truth. I know quite a bit about your kind, but this? I wouldn't even know where to start."

Well, this is a first...

"It certainly is, Miss Addison."

My cheeks burned because, of course, I had said that out loud. As I watched the sheriff walk away, my throat suddenly dried and filled. I wasn't sure what I was expecting, but not being interrogated was not it. I had gotten so used to Romero's gruff and strict exterior, I didn't know what to do with the version of him that trusted me fully.

"Oh, and Miss Addison?" the sheriff called from the open doorway. "I don't have to tell you two not to leave town. You haven't been cleared in Mr. Hunt's case and we need to keep up appearances. The coroner ruled the death as a heart attack, but now that I have heard your side of the story, I'm going to check on a few things. Let's keep each other abreast."

There he was. I nodded. Joe gave the sheriff a little salute. We stayed behind a few more minutes to process what happened before ducking out of the room and rushing out of the station. The first thing I noticed when we finally made it outside was how much colder it had become since we went in. The second, and likely most terrifying, thing I saw were the ghosts surrounding the police station. There had to have been at least twenty of them crowding the parking lot and looping all the way around the side of the building.

I swallowed, using my feet to bury my weight deeper into the pavement.

As on several previous occasions, the ghosts did not speak. Their limp lips opened and closed lazily, no sound coming out. I nudged Joe's side, whispering, "Ghosts. A lot of them," out of the side of my mouth.

"Where?"

I pointed to the large gathering of spectral forms. It was then that another source of magical energy caught my attention. Behind the ghosts, half hidden behind the wall of the police station, was a large, glowing rift. An opening to the Underworld. I sneered.

My father wanted a word.

Checking to make certain Stella didn't use this particular time to make an appearance, I started for the opening. Joe stayed close behind me, his body heat pressing me forward. As we neared the ghosts, they parted like the sea, letting us come through. Near to me, Joe kept his gaze on the rift, but once in a while I caught him glancing around, his brow thick with worry. He couldn't see the ghosts, of course, but that didn't mean he didn't feel out of place here. Who wouldn't?

A tightness formed in my bones as we got closer to the rift—the Underworld calling for me to come home. I fought the urge to jump in with every step. My fingers coiled around Joe's sweater and I held to it with a vice grip like a lifeline.

"I got you," Joe said.

He didn't even get a chance to close his mouth when another voice boomed over to us. One I had come to despise thoroughly.

"The time is near, daughter dearest," my father, Hades, hissed from inside the rift.

I rolled my eyes. "Still with the theatrics, I take it? What do you want?"

"Considering your upcoming sacrifice, I will let your disrespect go unnoticed this time," Hades warned. "I am simply making sure my investment is ready."

Seriously, Mom. How did you stand this guy?

I shook off whatever thoughts that followed my mother and Hades dating before I vomited on the ground. My throat tightened, and I worked hard to hold on to my bravery. My eyes narrowed on the rift. "First of all, note the disrespect. There is more where it came from, and I meant every word. Secondly, I am not giving up my life for you. So stop bothering me."

The rift expanded quickly, and Joe and I had to jump backward to keep from colliding with it. Around us, the ghosts screamed silently, their gray bodies moving closer to box us in. I clung to Joe, my hands trembling against my will.

"Enough!" Hades shouted. As his voice rose, the rift vibrated with all of his power and energy. "Two weeks. I will see you in two weeks and you will fulfill your destiny. Or I will take everyone you love without a second thought."

Joe growled deep in his chest and I had to shift my body to come between him and the rift before he acted in a way he'd regret later. My head shook to tell him to back down, relief flooding my body when he listened. Before us, the rift widened again, and a strong, magnetic force burst from within. It tore past us, reaching for the souls gathered here. Its icy fingers grabbed each ghost with a hunger I couldn't explain and yanked them back inside, back into the Underworld. Terror flashed over their deadly features as they vanished into the rift. When the last of the ghosts was pulled in, the rift shut, a zipper closing.

I slumped against Joe's chest.

"What just happened?" he asked.

Sweat rolled off me in panicked waves. "We need to figure out another way to track the ritual site. Map or no map, it needs to happen now. We are out of time."

CHAPTER 7

The knife sliced across the thick, buttery pancake with a satisfying sound. I used my fork to push the piece out of the way before moving on to cut the next one. Thoughts swirling in my head, I continued to cut my breakfast into small bites, but I was entirely elsewhere. No matter how hard I tried to ignore the dread of epic proportions tearing a hole in my gut, I couldn't get myself to move past it.

"Have I missed something?" Stella asked, pointing to the tiny slices of pancake filling my plate. "Is there a toddler you're saving that for?"

I shoved the plate away with a groan. "Ugh! He makes me so mad I can't stand it!"

"I'm assuming we're not talking about the imaginary child right now."

"Hades," I told Stella, taking a sip of my London Fog Latte. The taste of tea and honey hit the back of my throat and for a second, I almost completely forgot about my nightmare of a life. "He is seriously deranged if he thinks I'm going to sit back and let him use me as a vessel to cross over."

With a fast whoosh, the ghost slid across the room. Stella pushed herself up on the counter to sit in front of me, her long, slender legs crossing. Leaning back on her hands, she regarded me with the same look Gran used to give me when she couldn't figure out what I was thinking. "And you counted twenty ghosts?"

"I mean, not exactly." I shrugged. "But it was a lot. They filled half the parking lot for coffee's sake. Why do you think he brought them out? To get my attention?"

"Or to show you how much power he has over souls, even from beyond the rift," Stella suggested.

"Well, whatever he wanted, he sure got on my last nerve."

I pushed away from the counter and walked to the sink, dumping my plate in. There was no way I'd be able to eat anytime soon. Even if I did desperately need the energy.

The air shifted as Stella whirled off the counter

and floated to the living room. She made it from one side of the room to the next, emulating pacing to the best of her ghostly abilities. "So, what are we thinking?" she asked.

"About what?"

"Don't be obtuse, Piper," the ghost scolded me. "The map guy. Who do you think did him in?"

I gripped hard on the stone countertop. "The coroner said it was a heart attack."

"You can't possibly believe that."

The stone nearly cracked with how hard I was squeezing. Leave it to Stella to pinpoint exactly what had me up in knots in T minus thirty seconds. The ghost knew me better than I knew myself.

A grin tugged at my lips. "That's it!" I yelped excitedly. "Something was eating away at me and I kept thinking it was the whole Hades situation. Which, don't get me wrong, sucks. But it was what happened to Leon that bugs me, I think."

"I mean, I could have easily told you that before."

"We get it, you're brilliant," I said to the ghost, finally peeling myself from the countertop. I made my way to the living room and fell into the plush cushions of the couch, swallowed by them almost entirely. "If it was a heart attack, why was Leon holding his talisman when he died? The way we found him looked like he was about to reach for his magic and was too late."

"And you don't know what type of paranormal he was?"

I shook my head. "No, but I'm guessing a warlock. Joe couldn't smell vamp or werewolf on him. Granted, he could be one of the lesser common paranormals, though I doubt it. Not too many of them around these days."

"Strange he didn't use his magic if he was under attack."

That was bizarre. The thought had crossed my mind briefly when we left the Inky Atlas. Why did Leon not fight back? It was possible his energy was drained, and he hadn't yet had a chance to recoup it from the ley lines running under the town. Warlocks needed those lines after using magic or it took them forever and a day to work up their magic reservoir again. It was one thing that separated them from witches who could pull energy from earthly things. It was also why the two didn't get along all that well.

So, yes, there was a small chance that Leon didn't have enough magic to fight his assailant. But that didn't explain the talisman. Surely there was some energy in his family's power source he could pull from.

Unless...

I zeroed in on Stella's pale gray eyes. "What if he didn't know he was about to die?"

"As in, someone snuck up on him?"

"As in magic did," I corrected. "What if a Sister used dark magic to kill Leon and take the map so we couldn't find it?"

Stella mused over my theory, continuing her floating in the living room. At this rate, she would start a mini wind storm if she didn't slow down. When she finally stopped moving, I breathed out the breath I didn't realize I was holding.

The ghost's face sharpened, her high cheekbones rising. "You're assuming the coven knows you're after them. Didn't Sylvie say she's playing it safe?"

"She is. And they don't know about me," I explained. "But that doesn't mean they're not covering their tracks. Mom mentioned that the top witches are being extra secretive. It stands to reason they fear the location of the ritual might get out. If they knew there was a map that could help someone figure it out, I bet you the last of my coffee that they would want it gone."

"You're also assuming Leon had said map."

Shoot. Stella was right, I was reaching. The chances of anything I said being correct were so far-fetched it was laughable. Yet it was our only theory to work with, and I couldn't sit back and do nothing while the Blood Moon inched closer.

I pulled a throw over my legs, cocooning myself in

its warmth. "A lot of maybes, I know," I said. "but you have to admit, the timing is impeccable. Mom realizes that we need a map to track the ritual location and on the same night a warlock cartographer kicks the bucket? It's too much of a coincidence."

"Agreed," Stella said with a curt nod.

She floated toward the opposite of the living room. My head pounded. *Not this again.* When I realized she wasn't stopping, I followed her trajectory to the front door. With a shimmer, Stella vanished for a few seconds, reappearing before the doorway with a frustrated look on her face.

I watched her place her hands on her hips, her foot tapping silently. Not needing a further explanation, I groaned, tossed the throw from my legs, and swung them over the side of the couch. Climbing into my warmest coat, I zipped it up tight and threw on a pair of boots. As I turned the handle, I gave the ghost one quick glance.

"We need to call Joe too," I said. "He'd kill me if I broke into a crime scene without telling him again."

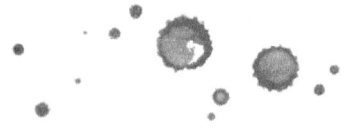

After some back and forth, I managed to convince Joe to stand guard while Stella and I snuck into Leon's home. At this point, the man was used to my stubbornness and realized it was either he was protecting us by keeping watch for cops or listening to an hour of me arguing. Little did he know, his job in this operation was the most important one, considering how many times I'd been busted sneaking into places.

Giving me a final kiss on the cheek, he stepped aside and watched as I disappeared into the darkness of the Inky Atlas, my red curls bouncing behind me. A few steps ahead, Stella floated on to inspect the shop. I couldn't be certain, but I could have sworn I heard her hum in excitement a few times.

Little weirdo.

"I'll take the shop, you check upstairs."

"Roger that," I said with a salute.

Stella's lips down-turned in disgust. "Please stop that."

Chuckling, I left the ghost to rummage through the main shop and took to the spiral staircase. This time around, the strange pull of magic I felt before was gone and I could actually breathe easy. The police must have taken the talisman pen with Leon's body for evidence or else I'd be heaving right about now. I made a mental note to ask Romero to inspect it later and kept moving.

Without the looming threat of finding Leon's dead body, the upstairs of the shop—Leon's home—was much cozier than I remembered. The overfilled book-cases that gave me slight claustrophobia last time seemed much more inviting, and I found myself perusing the titles on the spines, using the electric blue surge of my magic to light the space. Most of the titles had to do with mapmaking, which came as no surprise, but I was shocked to find that Leon had a significant collection of gothic romance novels. And even some mysteries to boot.

Reluctantly, I pulled away from the bookcase and inspected the remainder of the main living space. It was fairly normal, with no indication of a warlock living here. While it was the opposite of the farmhouse that had an entire room dedicated to witch work, not all paranormals practiced in their home. Warlocks, for example, didn't require items to use their magic, so it made sense I wouldn't find many hints of it here.

Not even a protective rune on the door? I'd have expected Leon to use his power for at least that.

A memory of the cartographer jumping in front of my car flashed before me. Perhaps Leon was strange in more ways than I realized at first.

After checking the kitchen, bathroom, and small bedroom, I found myself hesitating in front of the door leading to Leon's study. The body was gone, I knew that, but the memory of finding him in that chair stayed with me. My stomach grumbled as I reached for the handle and pushed the door open. I had to duck under crisscrossing yellow police tape to get inside, which did a great job of sobering me up. *Get in. Get out. Don't dilly dally.*

Pushing into the room, the first I noticed was how stuffy it was. The air was stale and settled in a way that made me struggle to take deep breaths. There was a smell I couldn't quite pinpoint, too, though considering that there was a corpse here not so long ago, I didn't press the issue.

I made quick work of checking the bookcases, then proceeded to the table. Giving it a good search, I came up empty fairly fast. The police did a better job clearing the crime scene this time around. There was literally nothing left to find.

Frustrated, I looped around to head back out. As I did, the light from my magic glimmered off the bottom of Leon's large antique desk, making me pause. I waved my hand, the light continuing to dance across a shiny surface.

My heart raced. There was a hidden compartment under the desk and my magic reflected off the hinges.

Dropping to all fours, I slid the tall armchair out of the way, cringing at the sound the clawfoot legs made as they scraped across the wooden floor. In one swoop of motion, I twisted to lie on the floor with my eyes checking the bottom of the desk.

"What were you hiding, map maker?" I whispered into the darkness.

My arm shot up, and I carefully traced the area where I saw the glimmer of metal. As I did, my skin cooled as the texture of the wood changed into the cool feeling of another surface.

"Aha!" I yelped.

Using the tip of my finger, I pulled at the well-concealed handle crafted onto the flat surface of the desk. As I did, the desk creaked and my eyes grew in size, watching a small compartment pop out. "Gotcha!"

Glancing at the open door, I reached into the hidden drawer and felt around. My shoulders slumped, and I yanked my arm back out, empty.

If there was a map in there, it was long gone now.

Sliding on my butt, I pushed out from under the desk and sat up. My face stopped two inches away from Stella's and I shrieked in surprise. Clutching my chest, I waved for the ghost to back up.

"For coffee's sake, Stella! Is personal space not a thing for you? You almost gave me a heart attack."

The ghost shrugged, unmoving. "Got anything?"

"Not a thing," I replied, scrambling to get up. I

dusted myself off and closed up the hidden compartment before facing my familiar. "How about you?"

"Our cartographer had an angry ex-girlfriend," Stella answered. "I found an email from her that sounded very heated."

My brow creased. "You hacked his computer?" Then, thinking about it more, added, "Why didn't the cops take it with them?"

"Heart attack, remember? I doubted they searched downstairs all that well. Anyhow, I didn't hack anything. I simply looked."

"Did it sound threatening?"

The ghost sneered, her gray skin stretching around the eyes and mouth. "She quite literally threatened to kill him, so I'd say yes, yes it did." She flipped her ponytail from one side to the other. "I got a name, so we should head out."

"Shouldn't we check more, see if we can find the map?"

"Definitely not."

My eyes narrowed and nerves tingled my skin. The hair on the back of my neck rose to stand. Stella wasn't saying everything. "What are you hiding?" I asked, suspicious.

"Nothing. But you should probably hightail it out of here," Stella said. "Joe has been trying to get your attention for the last five minutes."

Palm meeting forehead, I groaned in annoyance and walked to the only window in the room. My heart sank into my boots when I saw that I was too late. Standing beneath us in the same spot I left him was Joe. The moonlight danced off his tousled hair and I could see his muscled neck tense all the way from up here. All in all, I would have found this moment to be a wonderful reminder of how attractive my boyfriend was, except for one thing.

Joe wasn't alone.

CHAPTER
8

"What do we now?" I asked Stella, my voice barely a whisper. Below us, Joe made small talk with a stocky man in his mid-thirties. All I could see was the top of his beach-wave brown hair and a prominent nose that he kept pointing upward. Each time the man looked up, I ducked behind the curtain I hid near so as not to be spotted.

What was he doing here at this hour?

"I have an idea," my familiar said. She gestured to the door. "Let's go."

We trekked down the spiral staircase, my feet padding softly on the floor while Stella floated a foot ahead. When we reached the lower shop level of the building, Stella motioned for the door to the yard, then to the neighboring building. I followed her gaze, eyes working up to the surrounding darkness until I saw a passage similar to the one we took to get into Leon's in the adjacent shop.

Around the front, Joe's voice boomed as he spoke louder and louder, no doubt signaling me to stay away. I stopped trying to make out what he was saying and concentrated on following Stella as she led me away from the Inky Atlas and into dark oblivion.

The passage on this side was much narrower, with the rough, uneven brick walls scraping against my coat as I slid step by shaky step toward the main street. The air was thick with the damp, musty scent of old wet buildings and rust. Over my head, a pigeon cooed. I glanced upward, noting the dark, fluttering shapes perched on ledges high above, their eyes glinting in the moonlight. I prayed to the coffee gods that I wouldn't get hit by bird poop while already in an uncomfortable situation. My heart pounded in my chest, a mixture of nervousness and urgency pushing me forward. Each step seemed to stretch into eternity, the narrowness of the passage suffocating me with every move.

In front of me, Stella came to an abrupt stop, and I skidded to avoid sliding through her ghostly body.

"What is it?" I asked.

The ghost nodded to the street. "When I say so, get out there and pretend you just got here."

I nodded in agreement and waited for her signal. I didn't have to wait long. Before I knew it, Stella was flapping her arms and sounding out bird calls like a complete lunatic. Rolling my eyes, I jumped out of my hiding spot and onto the main street. The brick caught on my coat and ripped out a few threads in the process, a tear I'd have to worry about later. Brushing myself off, I walked at a casual pace down the street toward Joe and the stranger.

Seeing me approach with trepidation, Joe's brows slanted questioningly. I waved a hand. "Hey, there! Sorry I'm late. I got turned around looking for the place."

"Oh." Joe returned the wave with a wavering hand. "It's all right. Glad you finally made it."

I hurried up the walkway to the front of the Inky Atlas, pretending to see it for the first time. Peering inside, I scrunched up my nose and feigned confusion. "It looks closed." I turned to the man standing by Joe. "Are you here to buy a map too?"

"Piper, this is Drake Jenkins," Joe said with a faltering smile. "He's actually the landlord for the Inky Atlas. And I'm afraid it's been closed indefinitely."

Good job, Joe. Way to keep up the act. I smiled. We made a great team, him and I.

Extending a hand, I waited until Drake shook it before keeping up the charade. "You own the shop?" I asked. "What's this about it closing down for good? I thought Joe said the man running it had been here for years."

"About that..." the man's voice was higher pitched than I expected and it took me a second to connect it with his gruff face. He rubbed a calloused hand over his dark beard and looked between Joe and me with concern dotting his features. "There's been an incident. I'm afraid to be the one to break it to you, but Leon is dead."

Slapping a hand to my chest, I opened my mouth wider than it had any business being and stared him down. "Dead? What do you mean, dead?"

The landlord cleared his throat awkwardly. "Heart attack, I believe," he explained.

"What an absolute tragedy."

"Yeah, no kidding, lady," Drake said. His attitude was standoffish, but it was what he said next that had my ears burning. "I'll never get what's owed to me now."

My gaze darted to Joe, who tucked his chin into his chest. I peeled my teeth apart, but before I could say another word, Joe interrupted.

"Drake was telling me about the trouble he's had

with the map shop over the years before you got here," he exclaimed.

"Nice way of putting it," the landlord said bitterly. "Not to speak ill of the dead, but Leon was the worst tenant I've ever had. Never paid on time, always had an excuse for it. You know he owed me almost six months of rent for this place? Not to mention I let him have it at a steal when he first moved in."

I took a few steps so I could get closer to Joe and have a better view of Drake's face when he talked. One thing I learned after many instances of shoving my nose where it didn't belong was that every person had a tell. No matter how hard people tried, they always showed their true colors. Some hid it better than others—case in point, every killer that caught me off guard and put me in danger—but if I thought back on my original interactions with those people, there were signs I missed.

This time around, I wasn't taking any chances.

Not with the safety of the world on the line.

I looped my arm through Joe's and worked to appear as casual as possible. "I didn't know him, but Leon doesn't sound like a very nice man."

"He was fine," Drake said, sighing deeply. "A bit odd, but not a surprise considering how into maps the guy was. I'd like him a lot more if he paid his rent, though."

"I suppose map making isn't all that profitable."

A vein throbbed in Drake's neck and his eyes darkened. He flipped the collar of his leather bomber jacket up, shielding himself from the dropping temperature. Over our heads, a light dusting of snow swirled as Drake asked, "What did you need with Leon, anyway?"

"I'm a map collector myself," Joe lied. "Leon mentioned one I was interested in and when I told Piper about it, she said she'd love to see it, too. I wonder if someone will take over the shop with Leon gone. Would love to get my hands on the piece."

"Ha!" Drake coughed out. "Good luck with that. There's nothing left." His eyes widened as he realized what he said. "The police mentioned it earlier when I spoke to them. And I don't think Leon had any family in town. Not that I know of, anyway."

As Drake droned on about maps and shops, trying to change the subject, my mind swirled with a whirlwind of thoughts and suspicions. His voice, monotonous and cocky, filled the front of the Inky Atlas, but my attention was elsewhere. He probably didn't mean to do so, but it was too late now; my curiosity had been piqued. I highly doubted the cops told Drake anything about the missing maps. If I knew Romero—and by now, I felt I knew him all too well—he'd be keeping the details of the case tightly under wraps, hidden like a well-guarded secret. Romero was methodical and discreet, never one to let crucial information slip through the cracks. Why would the police tell the landlord of the map shop anything at all when the death was ruled natural? The question gnawed at me.

Unless there was another way that Drake found out about the missing maps.

Could he have come looking for them as a means of payment? As far as I could tell, there were two ways that scenario could have played out. Drake could have come to get his money from Leon. The two got into a fight and Drake killed Leon, stealing the maps for himself.

Option two, and the more likely one, was that Drake found Leon dead and took the maps before Joe and I got here.

Of course, there was also the chance that someone already raided the place like we originally thought.

My brain grew foggy with uncertainty. A moment ago, I was convinced that Leon was killed by the Sisters, but now...

I pulled away from Joe, excused myself, and walked to the end of the street. When I was out of sight, I pulled out my phone and pulled up the sheriff's personal cell number. He gave it to me ages ago, and I was really hoping he wouldn't regret it now.

Typing quickly, I sent him a message to ask if he looked into Drake Jenkins. I was about to pocket my phone and walk back to the shop when the screen lit up; my mom's number flashing in my face.

I accepted the call with a flick. "Mom? What's happening?"

"Hi, honey," she said, her tone warm and inviting on the other end of the line. "I have some great news."

My chest exploded with excitement. "Finally! Lay it on me!"

"After some intense interference from our ghost friend—don't ask—I was able to track down the map we needed. It's not the exact one the Sisters used for their coordinates, at least not that I think, but the year it was created is pretty close. I believe I can use a combination tracking spell on it to get us close. If not even dead on."

"That's amazing!" I screeched. Then, lowering my voice to a more human octave, added, "I hit a dead end on my end. You made my night. You have no idea how happy I am right now. So, where do we find this map?"

"That's the best part. It's in Orchard Hollow already," my mother said. "There's a shop called the Inky Atlas, and as far as their website says, they should have it in stock. Do you know the place?"

The night exploded around me. The once silent darkness was shattered by the howling wind, swirling snowflakes, and distant echoes of Joe and Drake's muffled conversation. My face hurt as snow fell on my cheeks, the cold crystals biting into my skin and cooling me down until I was frozen in place. The icy chill penetrated my bones, making it difficult to move. Eyes traveling down the street toward Leon's shop, I stood on weakened legs, barely staying upright.

The map we needed was in the shop, and now they were all gone.

How wonderful.

CHAPTER 9

S team billowed from the mugs I balanced on top of the tray, the smell of London Fog Lattes filling the cafe. I watched the mugs slide across the star pattern on the tray, a bead of sweat dangling from my brow. Five more steps. Four more steps.

Three.

Two.

One.

I set the tray on the table and breathed out in relief. One more order delivered without accidents; I was getting good at this.

"Table five is ready!"

Thanking the customers and leaving a stack of napkins behind, I turned back to Rory, who had prepared two more trays, all with their own piles of steaming mugs. My eyes landed on the clock. A few more hours and we can close up. My feet ached and my back felt like someone had run me over with a tractor. I was also quite sure that my hair was a hot mess, mostly because Stella made an appearance earlier and told me all about it.

Still, it was nice to stay busy.

In between hauling drinks and baked goods to the constantly rotating tables, cleaning up, and shooing Harry Houdini out of the doggy door Rory installed in the office—because why not make one for a raccoon—it was so hectic I barely had time to think.

What I did, however, was find plenty of time to check my phone. I glanced at it again, disappointed. Nothing from the sheriff yet.

Rory and I worked in tandem for the remainder of the day and well into the evening. With her on holiday break, it was great to share the workload, and the teenager had taken to spending more time at the cafe since she could practice magic here after hours. Since she was such a big help during the workdays, I didn't mind one bit. I even had a spare key made for her so she could come and go as she pleased. An act that earned me a fast hug, followed by a mumbled thank you. High praise from the kid.

The hours sped by as the two of us busted our butts to keep the lines short and the customers happy. Between the two of us, we made so many specialty drinks that I had to put in an emergency espresso bean order for tomorrow so we could keep the doors open. Holiday season in Orchard Hollow was no joke and even though we were over a month away from the big day, the town was already crawling with tourists.

It was a nice change of pace from the slower months we had prior.

I watched the last customer of the evening leave and tossed my apron on the counter. Sinking into a chair near the front windows, I watched Rory tidy up the espresso machine, then take off her own apron.

"Is it fine if I stay behind and practice tonight?" she asked.

I beamed at her. "Of course. I'm going to stick around and do some work as well. Come get me if you need anything."

With a thumbs up, Rory disappeared into the office. I pulled out my laptop and slid it on the table, getting ready to do some research on Drake Jenkins. If the sheriff wasn't going to come through, then I'd have to follow this lead myself. I had to clear Jenkins so I could figure out what happened to Leon. More importantly, I had to find out what happened to the maps.

If Mom was right, locating the map she mentioned was our best bet, and I had the distinct feeling that figuring out what killed Leon was going to lead me straight to it. No matter what the police thought, the man didn't die from a heart attack. I knew it and I was going to prove it.

Cracking my knuckles, I pulled up a fresh search tab and went to work. In the back office, the sound of Rory yelping each time a spell went awry kept a steady beat for my sleuthing. I smiled. Whatever this new phase of my life was, I liked it. My mood dimmed slightly. All the more reason to keep the world spinning on its axis.

The first few attempts at digging up dirt on Drake Jenkins proved useless. I unearthed a few social media accounts that were fitting for the man. That is to say, they were all equally self-indulgent with a lot of pictures of him taken in front of a mirror. There was an article in a local paper a few towns over about a location Drake opened for rent and when I pulled it up, it looked similar to the building Leon rented from him. A few more searches and I found out that Drake closed the place a year ago after several failed attempts to have it rented.

No wonder he was desperate to get his back rent from the cartographer—Drake was probably out of a lot of money from his failed business venture.

"All the more reason to kill," I whispered.

"Kill who?"

Gasping, I slammed the lid of the laptop shut and looked up. Hovering above me was Cilia Craven. Her wavy blond bob hung in flawless tendrils over her face and she watched me with sparkling interest in her eyes. I was so enthralled with my research I didn't hear her come in.

Heart regaining normal speed, I expelled a breath through my teeth. "You scared me," I said. "Here for Rory?"

Cilia took off her long wool coat and hung it over the back of the chair across from me. Not waiting for an invitation, she sat down and fixed me with one of her signature glares. The ones that meant business. "My manager duties at the hotel are done. I figured I'd wait until she's done with practice." Her shoulders rolled, and she sat up straight as a pin. "You didn't answer my question."

I sighed.

"Have you heard about Leon Hunt yet?"

"The map guy?" Cilia asked.

Clearly, Orchard Hollow was faster at spreading

news than a gossip column. I nodded. "Yes, him. Would it surprise you if I said I don't think his death was naturally caused?"

"Coming from anyone else?" Cilia asked. "Yes. But you? Not at all. Why do you think that? Actually, let me guess. This is about the Sisters of the River."

Over the last little while, Cilia and I have gotten closer. Enough so that I considered her one of my very closest friends. When I told the witch about my peculiar familiar, she was delighted and said being tethered to a ghost suited me perfectly. After finally caving in and letting her in on the secret of my magic, and the coven, with Mom's approval, of course, Cilia offered to help in any way she could. I hadn't taken her up on that yet, choosing to keep her at a distance from the nastiness that was Hades and the Sisters. It was good to have someone else to talk to about this stuff. Joe, Stella and my mother were great, but Cilia had a brand of straightforwardness that I enjoyed. One that always helped clear my head.

I opened up the laptop again and turned it to face her. "That's the thing," I said. "I'm not sure. Leon had a talisman on him when he died and I'm assuming he was a warlock. But there were no other signs of magic on the scene. And before you ask, yes, I was the one who found him. Well, me and Joe."

Cilia laughed.

"What?"

"Oh, you know what they say," she teased. "The couple that finds dead bodies together..."

I stretched to punch her arm lightly. "Anyway. My mom said that Leon had a map in his shop that could help us narrow down the ritual location, but the thing is, when we were there, there were almost no maps around. He had a few of the touristy ones and maps that looked like replicas but nothing that might actually be worth a lot of money."

"And you're entertaining the idea that a Sister killed him to get rid of the map."

"It's possible," I said. "Except why steal every other map in there? Why not take what you need and go? Surely a Sister would know which map she needed."

A dark red nail tapped on the tabletop as Cilia thought my words over. I pointed to the screen with the article on Leon's landlord pulled up and zoomed in on the part about him losing the business. "When Joe and I came back to the map shop, we met this guy. He gave off the impression that he wasn't too happy with Leon. Though I wouldn't be either if someone was refusing to pay rent for months on end."

"Do you think he was angry enough to take matters into his own hands?"

"That's what I'm trying to figure out," I admitted.

"Stella thinks Leon's ex-girlfriend is worth looking into, but I haven't had a chance to check it out yet."

The nail continued its dance. Tap tap tap. Tappity tap tap. I gave Cilia some time to wrap her head around all the information I'd dumped in her lap, biting on my bottom lip while I waited. Finally, she let out a whistle, grinning at me mischievously.

"Any reason you're not going to the sheriff with this?"

I cocked my head to the side. "He won't get involved if it's a paranormal matter. I think the last few unexpected deaths in town have him rattled."

"Right. Makes sense." Cilia pulled out her cellphone and gripped it tightly. "Do you know the ex-girlfriend's name by any chance?"

"Paityn Sawyer," I replied instantly. "Why?"

Not answering, the witch typed a long message into her phone and placed it on the table. "Give her a minute."

"Her?"

A moment after I spoke, Cilia's phone vibrated, running to the right like it was trying to escape. The witch snatched it up and flicked the screen, her eyes darting from side to side as she read. Anticipation thrummed in my veins as I waited for her to tell me what was going on. I bit the inside of my cheek, then proceeded to chew on my tongue for good measure.

"Your familiar has a keen sense for these things. She was right to point the finger at the ex," Cilia said.

I fidgeted in the chair that seemed extra stiff now. "Who did you text?"

"Nancy," she replied. "Who else? If you want dating gossip, no one knows more than her."

My mouth opened to object, but she stopped me before I could speak. "Don't worry, I didn't tell her any of the details." Rereading the message, she flashed me her phone and said, "Nancy says Leon was a terrible boyfriend. Left Paityn for another woman then accused her of stealing from him. According to Nancy, it left Paityn enraged." She pointed to the text again. "Her words, not mine."

I motioned for the phone and read the message when Cilia handed it over. As I read, I could hear Nancy's voice in my head and tried not to grind my teeth into dust because of it. Much as I couldn't stand the woman, she came through today. This was not information I could have easily gotten on my own, and I was grateful Cilia had thought of it.

It turned out it really did take a village. To solve a murder, that is.

Handing Cilia her phone back, I turned the laptop around, searching for another name this time. As results for Paityn Sawyer popped on my screen, my legs drummed under the table. Thoughts racing, I played out scenarios as I dug deeper to find out more about Leon's ex-girlfriend. Paityn may have been enraged about the accusation, but that didn't mean it wasn't true. What if she did steal from the cartographer in the end? And what if what she stole was my map?

CHAPTER 10

Cilia Craven

I left Piper to her online stalking under the guise of forgetting important paperwork in the hotel. She was so busy switching between the million tabs she had opened to even notice me gone, which suited me just fine right now. The less red flags I raised, the better.

Shutting the cafe door behind me, I glanced across the street. The Rose Hollow Hotel silhouetted against the setting sun cast dark, ominous shadows on the pavement, reaching almost as far as my feet. Fitting for a hotel that prided itself on false hauntings and ghost stories. Despite my best efforts after taking over the place, I was yet to get rid of the hotel's past. Though if I was being honest, I wasn't in too much of a hurry to do it. Ghosts kept the rooms booked.

A family with three young children pushed their giant suitcases through the wide front doors. I watched silently as one of our most recent hires, Joshua, hurried outside to help them, a smile on my face. The place ran itself for the most part now, leaving me plenty of time to plan for the future. Unlike Isabella, I had big ideas for our little slice of Orchard Hollow. Ones I hadn't shared with anyone yet.

All in due time.

Taking a peek at Piper through the cafe's window —deep at work—I stepped out of sight and got lost in the evening bustle of Cliff Row. Around me, voices mixed together and signs clanged as business owners closed up for the day. I watched Sunny exchange heated words with Ray and couldn't help but laugh. Things were never boring in our little town.

When I was certain Piper couldn't see me or over-hear the conversation, I slid my phone out of my coat and dialed.

The line rang three times before a familiar voice answered. "Go for Nancy."

"Hi, Nancy," I said, my voice hushed. "Cilia Craven here."

The witch mumbled to someone on her end, and the sound of loud footsteps echoed in my ear. A moment later she said, "Hi, Cilia. Sorry about that. I'm wrapping up at the salon."

No matter what people said about Nancy Steeles, the woman did hair like it was nobody's business. She was solely responsible for the bob I had been sporting for years. I wouldn't trust anyone else within an inch of my locks. I knew Nancy wasn't without her faults. No one was in our town, and she could be downright vindictive when it came to Piper, but man, hair was her thing.

I twirled a strand around my finger, checking behind me to make sure Piper didn't decide to follow me out. "No problem," I said. "I won't keep you long."

"Is everything all right? Is this about coven business?"

Nancy's voice lowered a few octaves when she mentioned our coven. The witch was often fairly vocal about magic, but her carefulness told me she wasn't alone and likely surrounded by humans. Choosing not to put her on the spot any further, I sucked in a breath and got down to business. "It is somewhat about the coven. And about the message I sent earlier."

"The one about the map guy and his ex?" Nancy asked, clearly confused.

"That's the one," I replied. "Look, I don't want you

to worry, but the coven might be in for a fight in the near future. I wanted to call and give you a head's up so you can get the girls ready."

I was met with complete silence that lasted for what seemed like forever. If I knew Nancy Steeles, she was either trying to make sense of what I said before speaking or already texting everyone and their mother to spread the news. I was really hoping it was the former.

After a few more breaths, Nancy said, "What's going on, Cilia? Are we in danger?"

"I'm not yet sure," I answered truthfully. "There are things happening that I can't speak to yet. It isn't my place. But if it comes down to it, I need to know that the coven will have my back. It is important."

Another brief moment of silence had me panicking. I very rarely lost my cool, but for some reason, the interaction with our coven's head witch had me going. One thing I had complete faith in was that I very rarely asked anyone for help and Nancy had to know that if I did, it was for good reason.

Luckily, I wasn't wrong.

"Of course you can count on us," the witch said. "We're basically family, Cilia. You know the girls will be there for whatever you need."

A smile tugged at my lips. "Thank you, Nancy. I

won't keep you longer, but be ready. If I call again, it's go time."

"So dramatic," Nancy replied with a high pitched, nasally laugh. "But you got it. Talk soon and stay safe. See you at the next ritual."

Satisfied, I hung up the phone, tightened the belt on my coat, and made my way back to Bean Me Up. Rory should be done soon and I didn't want her to wait any longer to get picked up. Her mother would murder me if I made the kid stay out late practicing magic when she could have been at home with her family. Not that I couldn't take my sister-in-law on. I scoffed at the thought, but sped up, regardless.

No point starting a fight over nothing. Not when there were real battles to be won.

As I neared the cafe, I noticed Piper was exactly where I left her. Her shoulders hiked up so high they were grazing the bottom of her ears. My poor friend was in over her head. I hated that she was tasked with such a massive responsibility. Being a paranormal was hard enough; being one that was related to an evil mastermind wanting to destroy your entire world was quite another.

I watched her whisper incoherently under her breath as she concentrated on the lit up laptop screen illuminating her face. Gaze darting to the phone in my hand, I tossed it back in my pocket and straightened out my spine.

"Don't worry," I whispered into the night. "You're not alone in this."

And it was the goddess given truth, wasn't it? No one was alone in Orchard Hollow. Not even when one really wanted to be.

CHAPTER 11

Paityn Sawyer's home was nestled in a part of town frequented often by tourists. Because the street faced the sea on one side, the homes were often rented out by homeowners during summer and brought in a gallop of people to the area. Today, though, with a light frosting of snow already on the ground, there was almost no one around.

I walked silently, my feet carrying me forward with trepidation. To my left, the sea angrily crashed to shore, and each wave seemed to envelop me in a chill that I couldn't shake. I had yet to hear from the sheriff and to make matters worse, Joe was too busy at the bookshop to join me in my hunt today. It took some convincing to get him to stay put and not to worry; a feat I was quite proud of.

Now, however, I wished I had taken him up on the offer to wait until he was done, so I didn't have to do this alone. What if my guess was right and Paityn was involved in Leon's death?

I shook my head. No point turning back now. I was already here, and it wasn't like I hadn't faced much worse before.

To be on the safe side, I summoned my magic, keeping it right below the surface of my skin in case I needed the help.

As I walked, I couldn't help but gape at the houses on Paityn's street. Each one was a marvel of color and quirky architecture that gave the homes personalities of their own. I passed one house with four chimneys, all painted in different shades. Another house had a winding cobblestone path that the owners chose to decorate to mimic a train track, complete with several trains to boot. A third home was painted the color of a flamingo and stood out like a sore thumb against its less bright neighbors.

My eyes widened with glee at the absolute wonderland unfolding before me.

Up ahead, I saw the numbers of Paityn's home discovered after a long night of researching and slowed my step. The home was one of the less extreme buildings on the street, yet it wasn't without its charm. The front yard overflowed with trees of every size, each one hosting rows of hanging lanterns at alternating heights. Under the lanterns, a wrought-iron table and chair set took up the majority of the vast space, resembling a tea party from a children's fairytale. I half expected a rabbit with a pocket watch to jump out at me as I turned into the walkway leading to the house.

The brick-laid path clicked under my feet as I inched closer to the two-story cottage. To my right, I noticed a shiny luxury car sitting in the driveway; the windows fogged up. Paityn must have returned home recently.

My chest tightened as I took the first of three steps at the base of the porch. Around me, more greenery lined the home as planters filled up the front porch. There were so many of them, it was almost over-whelming. A real jungle, if you asked me.

Steadying a shivering hand, I raised my knuckles to the red door and gave it a good, hearty knock.

"Coming!" a light voice yelled on the other side. It was followed by hasty footsteps and the sound of a dog barking. A big one, I'd wager. A second later, the door opened to reveal a beautiful woman in a knitted track-suit the color of the sky. She trained her golden eyes on me, her brow creasing. "Hi, there."

Bouncing behind the woman was a big, fluffy

retriever. She tried her best to contain him, finally giving up and letting the dog run past us into the front yard. It did a few circles around the table I saw earlier, then settled under a massive oak tree with content. The woman retied the thick, curly ponytail on her head and faced me again. "Sorry about him. He gets excited when I get home from work. What can I do for you?"

"Are you Paityn Sawyer, by any chance?" I asked, already knowing the answer.

The woman nodded, but I saw a glint of regret in her eyes. Was she scared of me? Was I scary? I checked my hands to make sure my magic wasn't escaping and plastered on my most welcoming smile.

That seemed to do the trick because Paityn relaxed again and said, "That's me." She tucked a loose curl behind her ear, her bronze skin shimmering in the light of the setting sun behind me. "I'm sorry, but do we know each other? I'm drawing a blank."

"Oh, no, we don't," I replied. "I'm really sorry to barge in like this. My name is Piper Addison, and I was hoping I could ask you about someone you knew that recently... passed away."

Paityn drew back inside by an inch. "Do you mean Leon?"

"Yes. Again, very sorry. I promise it won't take long."

Her eyes went to the dog, then darted back to me.

"All right," she said, opening the door a tad wider. "Give me a second to get Tinker inside the house."

I stood back and let Paityn walk past, making a straight line for the dog. As she wrestled the furball back inside, I couldn't help but giggle. The charade was oddly similar to what I had to do with Harry except, in our case, I was usually trying to get him out of the house, not back in it. The dog, Tinker, fought tooth and nail until Paityn reached into her pocket and pulled out a handful of dog treats. She let the dog shove his wet nose into her palm, yanked it away, and ran back toward me.

With a whoosh, Paityn darted past and into the home, the dog on her heels. I got hit by a large, strong tail and had to squeeze myself into the porch railing to make sure I didn't get bulldozer'd by the greedy pup.

A moment passed and Paityn was back outside, firmly shutting the door behind her.

"The only thing that works," she said.

"Don't I know it!"

She gazed at me through narrowed eyes. "You have dogs?"

"Raccoon, actually," I admitted. Then, realizing how wild that sounded, added, "It's a long story."

"Right. You said you wanted to ask me about Leon? I should mention I haven't spoken to him in months. Not since..." she trailed off. "Well, no matter now. Terrible what happened to him."

I arched one brow at her. "Did you mean since you two broke it off?"

"That's one way to put it," Paityn answered bitterly.

"What happened, if you don't mind me asking?"

Waving a palm at me dismissively, the woman scratched her long neck, her attention lost somewhere past my shoulder. A darkness spread over her features; one that would have made anyone else appear sinister, but it made Paityn even more beautiful. Ethereal, even. I attempted to reach out with my magic to see if I could sense any paranormal on her or a talisman nearby, but came up empty.

Paityn's beauty was all hers. No magic involved.

"I don't know how you knew Leon," she started, "but assuming you're from town, you'd have heard what happened. We were together for years, then he got up and left me out of the blue for another woman. One that has had it out for me since college, if you can believe it."

My jaw gaped. I really could not imagine that at all. The thought of Joe leaving me for, say, Nancy Steeles was laughable at best and absolutely horrifying at worst. I felt for Paityn for having been subjected to that treatment. That was until I remembered why I was here.

Pressing my lips into a thin line, I folded my arms over my chest, the zipper of my coat digging into me. "I may have heard something along those lines. It must have made you pretty angry with him."

"That's an understatement. I could have killed Leon."

Did you?

Paityn must have realized how that sounded, because she quickly corrected herself. "I didn't. Obviously."

"Of course not."

But perhaps you did?

"Anyhow, what he did wasn't as bad as him accusing me of stealing his dumb maps. Can you believe that?" She scoffed. "Me? Steal from him? Does it look like I need money?"

I looked at her and at the expensive car in the driveway. She had a point. Homes on this stretch of the town were worth a fortune, and judging by Paityn's appearance and the car she owned, I couldn't imagine any reason for her to steal. Definitely not maps, for that matter. How much could those go for, anyway?

"I always told him he needed a safe in that shop.

Some of those maps were worth quite a bit, you know?"

Oh. I smiled sheepishly. "I didn't realize it was such a lucrative business."

"It certainly could be," Paityn said. "At least it was for Leon. He had a hunch about these things. Always knew where to find the best maps and how to wrestle them away from their owners at a lower price. The man was good at what he did. I'll give him that. Now dating—that was a whole other story."

"I take it he wasn't the best boyfriend."

Leaning on the wall, Paityn loosened the band holding her hair hostage, and it fell in a cloud over her shoulders. "That was the thing. He actually was a great boyfriend. It was why I was so shocked when he left me, for Aisha Lang, of all people. Now if anyone was going to steal from him, it was her."

"Aisha is your college friend?" I asked.

"College nemesis," Paityn corrected. "Always had her nose where it didn't belong and a complete gold digger. Even back then, she only went for guys who had money. I'm surprised Leon went for her, honestly."

The arch in my brow heightened. "Was Aisha using Leon for money?"

"She definitely wasn't into him for his intellect," Paityn said snarkily. "A month after they started dating, she was dressed in all designer, drove a better car, and moved to a bigger apartment. The woman hasn't held down a job in decades. How was she able to afford all that?"

"With Leon's help," I whispered.

A finger shot up in front of me. "Exactly. But doesn't matter much now, does it? Like I said, it's a shame what happened, but I haven't spoken to him in some time. If you want to know anything specific, I can point you to a family member." Her eyes burned into me, stopping me stock still. *Do I have a woman crush?* "Better yet, you should talk to Aisha. Tell her I sent you. She'd love that."

The sound of whining and scratching interrupted us and Paityn winced, her attention on the front door. She pushed away from the wall to walk past me, her fingers grazing the handle. "I should probably get back before he destroys the house." She glanced at me over her shoulder before going inside. "Word of advice, dogs make for much better boyfriends. Take it from me."

As we said our goodbyes, I waited for Paityn to lock up before turning on my heels and heading back to the street. Taking a leisurely stroll, I made my way toward where I parked the car, walking much slower this time. The sea continued to barrel into the shore and yet the crashing waves didn't bother me anymore.

Instead, they played a soothing melody while I formulated my plan.

The interaction with Paityn bothered me and it wasn't until I was halfway up the street that I realized what it was. She was not a paranormal. I was convinced that magic had to be involved in the cartographer's death, but it was more than that. Leon Hunt was a warlock, and they were a snobby bunch. I couldn't picture a warlock dating a human, at least not for long. What if he didn't choose Aisha for the reasons Paityn thought?

Aisha may have been a gold digger but was there also a chance she was more than human? And if she had magic, perhaps she used it to do worse to Leon than simply drain his bank account.

CHAPTER 12

irt and broken pottery lay in heaps at the bottom of the greenhouse shelves. I stared in disbelief, my entire body vibrating. My teeth scraped against each other as I worked to get a hold of some patience.

"How did he manage to do this?"

The greenhouse was overturned. A chaotic mess spread through the once tidy space, making it look like a natural disaster tore through it. I cast a gloomy gaze at the tiny paws sticking out from beneath a scratched up blanket in the corner. I supposed a natural disaster did strike here after all.

"Seriously, Harry," I said to the hiding raccoon, "why?"

In response, Harry Houdini chittered away as he dug yet another hole in the ground under the greenhouse bench.

Floating above him, Stella cocked her hips with dramatic flair. "You should report the mailman for constantly delivering the furry bioweapon to your door."

"You may be right," I said, my jaw tight. "Why is he so obsessed with causing havoc?"

As if waiting for his chance to shine, Harry interpreted that to be the perfect moment to show me exactly how much havoc he could create. Using his back legs for momentum, he shimmied off the ground with surprising agility, kicking up a flurry of dirt and tangled plant roots into my face. I jumped back with a yelp, my eyes stinging and my vision obscured by the debris. The clothes I had carefully chosen this morning were now splattered with cold, half-frozen mud. Harry, on the other hand, was not bothered in the least. He took a brief interlude to turn himself around, looked at me with a mischievous glint in his eyes, and continued to dig. Around him, the once serene greenhouse stood as a battlefield, with clumps of earth laying everywhere and the neat rows of plants I had finally managed to keep alive uprooted and askew.

If Gran was alive, she'd be chasing the rascal down with the pointy end of a broom right now.

"What is he looking for? Geez."

"Maybe he's mining," Stella suggested.

I smirked. "For Balas Rubies?"

We burst out laughing at my foolish reference to the caves last week. Stella must have been as tired and delirious as me because no way should that comment have been so funny. Yet, here we were, slapping our thighs and wiping tears from our eyes. Cackling. Could ghosts get tired?

The random thoughts rushing through my head made me regain my composure. I trained my focus on the digger, stomping toward him at increasing speed.

Hearing my loud footsteps, Harry's ears perked up. He stopped what he was doing, scurrying in place before running out of the hole in the wall he used to get in. I shook my head. Searching the greenhouse, I found the largest pot not yet shattered and dragged it over with huffing breaths. Taking my time, I positioned it to block the hole as best as I could. "That should keep him out for a while."

"If only there was a pot large enough to cover the entire house," Stella retorted.

I brushed off the dust from my hands and inspected the damage. All in all, it wasn't as bad as I originally thought. A few broken containers, and some dug up plants, but nothing that I couldn't salvage with time. Settling down on my knees, I grabbed a trough and began to shovel dirt to cover the hole Harry dug up. As I reached out to dump the first pile, unearthed tree roots caught my eye. They intertwined beneath the soil, fighting each other for room to grow. One of the trees outside must have stretched out further than I realized and had begun to encroach on the earth beneath the greenhouse.

My gaze traced over the intricate pattern. It looked so familiar, almost like... "Ley lines," I whispered.

"What was that?" Stella asked.

"The ley lines," I repeated. "How didn't I not think of them before?"

The ghost looked me straight in the eye and said, "You've finally lost it, haven't you?"

I used the edge of the trough to uncover more of the roots, then stood up. At this height, I had a bird's eye view of the pattern and the more I looked, the more I realized how much the tree roots resembled the magical streams of energy running under our town. No wonder witches loved to work with plants; everything was somehow connected in the end.

Pointing to the pattern, I pressed my lips together, head cocking to the side. "What if we tap into the ley lines and use them instead of a map?"

"That sounds like it would require a lot of magic," Stella countered.

"But it could work." I scratched the back of my head, thinking. "There is a lot of power under this town and we could manipulate it to our needs. I'd have to check with Mom, but I think we could use the lines as a locator."

"How?"

My heart raced as I tried to think of a way to explain what I was thinking. It was such an out there idea that I didn't have the right words to clarify it. Especially since my knowledge of magic wasn't exactly scholarly.

"I believe if we had enough energy, we could get the ley lines to lead us to other sources of powerful magic. Almost like dowsing rods."

Floating to stand before me, Stella pouted, her brows squishing together in the center. "How far of a reach would it have? The ritual space could be anywhere in the country. Or the world."

"True," I agreed. "But it would have to be somewhere that has a connection to the Underworld. I'm willing to bet that wherever the ritual location is, it's somewhere close to a large surge of magical energy."

Stella stilled. "Maybe directly on top of another set of ley lines."

"Yes! You understand. It could be nothing, I know, but it's at least a direction to follow."

I left the tree roots exposed and headed outside. My brain raced with possibilities and I had to steady my excited heart before it sent me into cardiac arrest. Leaving Stella to ponder over my possibly insane plan, I rushed into the farmhouse.

I had to call Mom.

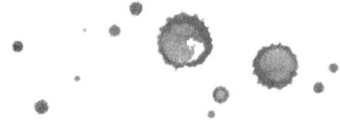

Two hours of trying to get through, and I finally got my mother on the phone. Apparently, she was having a disagreement with Isabella that turned into a full on food fight in Mom's small galley kitchen. I had no idea how one managed to fight with a ghost they couldn't actually see but leave it to Sylvie Addison to find a way.

The important part was that she gave me a thumbs up on trying to direct the ley lines to do our bidding and even suggested ways I could do so without needing a coven to amplify my magic. What it all came down to was giving the spell a target and, in this case, that target was me. Or my magic. Since Hades and I shared the source of our powers, Mom ideated that I could use the ley lines to track down any other similar magical signatures.

Unfortunately, the spell came with a warning. Shocker.

Not giving up too much of your energy because you never knew if there was another paranormal around who could accidentally absorb it. Since the last thing I wanted was to blast an innocent warlock with my Underworld magic, I needed to make sure that the area surrounding the ley lines was clear before trying anything.

Which was where Stella came in and why she was now sulking next to me as we trudged down the wild trails leading into the depths of the woods surrounding the farmhouse.

"What do I have to do again?" she groaned, her pale face standing out in the darkness of the surrounding trees.

I checked the notes I took earlier. "Nothing too difficult," I told the ghost. "I'll get set up and before I let my blood drop into the vein, you have to check a ten-mile radius and report back. If you see another paranormal, we don't do anything until they're gone."

"Is the blood truly necessary? You know how much I despise it."

I rolled my eyes. "Yes, I'm sure. I need to open a vein in the lines and give them something to track.

Then I direct their energy to a similar source of magic. Easy peasy."

"Lemon squeezy," Stella said automatically. Her eyes narrowed in disgust. "Ugh. You're rubbing off on me."

The trees got denser around us, branches packed so tightly almost no light made it through. Above my head, a flock of birds circled, their caws echoing in morbid synchronicity. In my veins, my magic rushed faster and faster. I stopped in my tracks. Looked at Stella. "I think this is a good spot."

Moving at the speed of light, or lack thereof, I followed Mom's notes to set up the circle. When I finished, I signaled Stella, who vanished, complaining under her breath the entire time. She returned in record time, reappearing before me and holding up a half-hearted thumbs up.

My breath caught in my throat as I brought the blade of the small kitchen knife I'd packed to my fingertip. Since the spell didn't require much blood, I was completely fine with a finger prick. Poking at my skin, I winced, fighting the urge to wipe the droplet of blood welling on my finger. With one glance cast in Stella's direction, I shoved my hand out and buried half my hand in the earth. It felt cool and clammy against my skin, and I cringed at the feeling of dirt digging under my nails.

We waited.

"Nothing is happening," Stella announced after five minutes.

My face contorted, scrunching until I was certain I resembled a Shar Pei puppy. "Maybe I didn't do it right."

"Or the location is out of reach of the ley lines."

I did not like that option. A part of me wished to fight with Stella; to tell her that she was dead wrong, and that we were going to stay here in the stupid woods and try until the spell worked. But another part, the rational one, knew there was a good chance she was right. It was quite possible that the reason nothing happened was because the ley lines didn't reach wherever it was the Sisters of the River hid their plans. With this little time left until the Blood Moon, they were certainly already in place, which meant the spell should have succeeded.

Except for the reason Stella said.

Groaning, I yanked my hand out of the ground and shook it off. Remnants of earth fell away in clumps and I had to look away, tears threatening to sting my eyes.

"Let's go home. We should—" I paused to look at my ringing phone. My eyes darted up to meet Stella's, then back to the screen. With a click, I picked it up and brought the phone to my ear. "Sheriff Romero. Hello."

Holding my breath, I listened as the sheriff spoke, not daring to interrupt. He spoke at a fast speed, his words clipped. It made me wonder if he was regretting making the call or if there were more pressing issues waiting for him to attend. *Dear goddess, don't let there be another body found.*

After the sheriff finished his monologue, I thanked him for calling me and hung up.

"Well? What did he want?" Stella asked.

I swallowed the gargantuan lump in my throat, clearing it for good measure. Gazing at my familiar, I chewed on my bottom lip. Uncertainty further ruined my already sour mood. "The lab results came back. Leon Hunt died from gas poisoning," I told the ghost. "We were way off. Magic had nothing to do with it."

CHAPTER 13

S o it wasn't magic. *Huh.*

I paced the aisles of Brooks Books, waiting for Joe to finish up with a customer. I have been up and down this aisle seven times now and if you had asked me to name one book, I'd draw a blank. Something about medieval history or maybe gardening. I had no clue.

Somewhere inside the shop, Joe directed another customer to a collection they asked for. His voice carried over the shelves and I found myself straining to listen. It wasn't important, of course, but eavesdropping helped me get back to the present moment and not dwell on what happened yesterday.

Not magic. Seriously?

Never in a million years would I have guessed that the cartographer who owned a map pointing to a magical place—one that was now conveniently missing—died of a fluke as basic as gas poisoning. In fact, I was so surprised by the sheriff's admission that I had to call him back after I took the time to process the information. The results were the same. Leon Hunt died from a leaking pipe that fed carbon monoxide into his poorly ventilated study.

I couldn't wrap my head around it.

My finger grazed the gilded edges of an old, worn-out spine. The title was barely legible, but judging by the condition of the book, I'd say my initial hunch about the section was correct. Unless Joe added an aisle devoted to medieval gardening, this had to be a history book.

Continuing to touch each spine, I walked toward the main area, my feet light. As I turned the corner, another section of the bookshop caught my attention and I paused, taking it in. The paranormal aisle.

To everyone else, this part of the shop was nothing more than fodder for tourists and magic enthusiasts, but those of us with actual power coursing through our veins knew better. Before dying, Joe's uncle had kept the bookshop stocked with all the latest tomes real paranormals might require. Anything from moon rituals for witches, blood alternative recipes for vamps, he even had a section on portal travel for fairies. I always found it odd considering how rare fairies were, and those that did manage to escape their horrid realm wouldn't dare open a portal to go back. But there you had it. Anything and everything magic was housed in a single aisle.

The aisle was magicked to hold more than meets the eye and some of the more delicate books were hidden from human perception. As far as anyone in town knew, a witch spelled the shelves as a favor for Joe's uncle. I, on the other hand, knew it was Gran.

She was always helping others.

"Thanks for coming," Joe said, close to my earshot. "Don't forget to grab a complimentary bookmark on your way out."

The front doorbell rang out as the customer exited. Right on cue, footsteps drew closer toward me as Joe left the register to come find me. His head poked around the shelf, catching me in the middle of petting another old book.

I dropped my hand to my side. "All done?"

"For now," Joe said. "I'm sure more will pop in soon."

"I suppose you're stuck here for the rest of the day," I said. "No chance of escape?"

Joe's face scrunched. "What are you up to?"

"The usual." I laughed, my face hurting from the

motion. "I was thinking about what the sheriff said. That Leon's death was an accident and had nothing to do with magic."

"And?"

Picking up a random book, I flipped through the pages. A slight wind kicked up from the paper and brushed against my skin. "And I don't buy it. But I also don't have any way of proving it. What I do have is a dead cartographer, missing maps, and a possible lead."

"Aisha Lang," Joe said. "Leon's new girlfriend. The one supposedly taking him for all he had."

I booped his nose playfully. "Bingo."

"Let me guess, you want to track her down?"

Shutting the book with a bang, I placed it back on the shelf, my eyes glimmering. "I kind of already have. Surprise!"

Joe's head shook and his shoulders followed suit. Rubbing his temples, he turned on his heel, marching away from me toward the front register. When he reached it, he turned around, returning my smile.

"Give me ten minutes to lock up and we'll head out."

My eyebrows rose. "What about the shop?"

"It'll survive," Joe replied. "I'm due for a lunch break, anyway."

"You don't eat," I reminded the vampire.

Locking up the register, Joe straightened out the

counter, then walked toward the wall nearest to him. He flicked a switch, casting the bookshop into darkness. In the glimmer of light pouring from the front windows, his eyes sparkled as he glanced my way. "Well, they don't know that, darling," he purred. "Let's go."

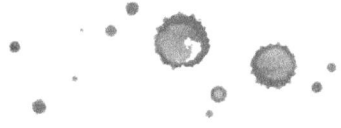

Tracking down Aisha Lang wasn't a difficult task. Unlike most people I knew, or had to stalk to get to, Leon's new squeeze loved social media. She had enough accounts to rival even the most popular influencers and was active in all of them. I had no idea where she found the time, frankly. I couldn't keep up with even one, which was why I chose not to spend any time there.

Though, if you asked my familiar, she'd tell you it was because I couldn't take a decent picture to save my life. Rude.

Unlike me, however, Aisha took great photos, and she had many of them. The one that interested me most was the picture she took this morning of her standing in front of the entrance to the Orchard Hollow Antique Market with the caption "Be here all day. See you around," posted under it. As we pulled into the vast and fairly empty parking lot of the event center, my eyes stayed glued to the sign above. The same one Aisha had in her photo. It turned out, it was fairly easy to find people when they put their entire lives online.

I climbed out of the passenger side of Joe's truck and landed on the pavement. Doing a quick scan of the place, I realized that it must have not been as busy today considering that the last time I was here, it was impossible to even find a parking spot. Granted, that was years ago and Gran and I came here on a weekend. And yet the antique market may have lost its charm, because I barely saw a soul as we made our way to the entrance.

"Probably much busier in the summers," Joe remarked, making the same observation.

I shrugged. "At least it'll be faster to spot Aisha if she's here."

We paid the small fee for a ticket and Joe held the doors for me to come in. As we entered, I was immediately hit in the face by the smell of nostalgia. Old books, old furniture, old everything. I loved it. I was never one for modern life, much to Stella's dismay, who had been begging me to upgrade the design in the farmhouse forever. But I knew I'd never cave. I loved having so much history in the place, it made it feel more like home.

Rushing to get further into the antique market, I understood that was why I liked coming here; it smelled of home.

Around us, booths of all sizes unfolded, each one boasting wares and knick-knacks that only the finest collectors would know how to spot. I noticed a table display of vintage tarot cards and another showing off a wide array of crystal balls and cauldrons. Paranormals were everywhere, even here at the market. Upon closer inspection, I realized that while the cauldrons and crystal balls were nothing more than cute, witchy decor, the tarot cards were the real deal, as was the witch selling them.

The urge to meander from one booth to the next and touch everything I could get my hands on pulled me forward, and I had to remind myself that we were not here for pleasure. Refraining from picking up a set of gemstone coasters, I looked at Joe. "We should come back another time to look around."

"Love to," he answered. Then, tugging my sleeve inconspicuously, he added, "I think I found your girl."

I followed where he was looking at a few booths away from us. Standing with her back to us was Aisha Lang. She wore the same pink hoodie she had on in the photo and her long, shiny hair would be unmistakable anywhere. Aisha had an air of effortless grace about her. Her posture was straight yet relaxed, giving off an air of confidence. Even from behind, you could sense her calm and collected demeanor.

After spending way too long staring at the woman, I noticed that the booth she was shopping at should have come as no surprise. "Are those maps?" I asked Joe.

"Antique ones from the look of it," Joe said with a nod. "Are you thinking what I'm thinking?"

I didn't reply, even though we were both on the same page. A few days after her boyfriend's death, Aisha Lang was pursuing old maps at an antique show. She didn't strike me as a cartographer or even someone who held any remote interest in the hobby, so why was she here? And why specifically at that booth?

Biting the inside of my cheek, I was trying to come up with a valid excuse to talk to her when Joe grabbed my hand and pulled me forward. We cleared the space between the booths as he whisked us toward Aisha with the determination and speed of...well...a vampire.. When we were right behind the woman, he turned to me, winked, and proceeded to collide directly with her back.

Aisha teetered forward, catching herself on the table with a grunt. As she turned, Joe put on a horrified expression that quickly melted away and turned into utter surprise. "Aisha?"

"Um, y-yes," the woman stuttered.

She obviously had no idea who we were, but that didn't seem to bother Joe, who was in his element now. Sometimes I wondered if he missed his calling as an actor. He pressed his hand to his chest, his jaw gaping open. "Leon's girlfriend, right?" he kept on. "We met at his shop a few months ago. I'm so sorry for your loss."

I watched in awe as Aisha's guard dropped before us. She put down the map she was holding, smiled at the vendor at the table, and turned to fully face us.

"Oh, right? Sorry, I must have forgotten," she said. "Things have been as you could imagine. Good to see you again..."

"Joe," my boyfriend offered. "This is Piper."

Aisha extended a slender hand. I shook it vigorously. "Nice to meet you. As Joe said, sorry for what happened. It's quite awful."

"Certainly it is," Aisha said. "Did you know Leon too?"

I shook my head. "Not as well as Joe," I lied. "But I was in the market to purchase a few maps and unfortunately didn't get to cross paths with him before he died. You must be devastated."

"Yes, definitely. Of course."

It was odd how the woman's words and actions didn't line up. Standing here in front of us with a face full of makeup, perfectly styled hair, and what I could only assume was a designer bag worth more than my entire wardrobe, Aisha didn't appear to be all that upset. And yet pain caught in between her words. A choked-out sob that only I could hear having fairly recently lost someone myself. When Gran died, I put on a very similar act and unless someone was looking intently, they'd never know that I cried for weeks on end.

Was Aisha really upset over the loss of Leon? If she was, it stood to reason she may not have been the one to kill him.

Gas poisoning, I had to remind myself. That was what killed him. Old habits die hard, or not at all in my case, because I couldn't help but search for a killer where there wasn't one.

No matter. I had to stay on track. We were here to find out if Aisha knew anything about the missing maps and nothing else.

I straightened my shoulders and stood up a little straighter. Pointed at the maps on the table and the hefty price tags attached to them. "I see you shared in his hobby."

"I... Oh. Sort of."

Hmm.

My eyes briefly flashed to Joe.

"Actually, Aisha," he said, "since you're here, maybe you'd be able to help us. Piper prepaid a lofty sum for a map she had her eye on right before the entire horrible accident, but wouldn't you know it? The police say Leon's shop was cleaned out. Like someone took all his maps. I was there a few weeks ago, and it looked fine to me. Do you know if Leon had another place where he stored orders?"

I smiled, adding, "It was an important piece to me, so I'd appreciate any help."

Before us, Aisha's confidence melted away. Her eyebrows met in the middle and her eyes jumped from side to side like she was looking for an escape route. She brought a bright pink nail to her lips, chewing on it nervously until the edges turned brittle.

Her panicked gaze landed on me. "The cops are looking for the maps?"

"They sure are," I said with fake confidence.

"Crap," Aisha whispered. She held onto the side of the table with white, shaking knuckles. Behind her, the vendor looked equally alarmed but I doubted it was for the same reason. "Double crap."

I ducked my head so I could catch Aisha's attention.

"Did you take them?" I asked at the same time as Aisha said, "It's not what you think."

I battled the need to look at Joe again, keeping my eyes trained on the woman. Her cheeks sank in and her mouth drooped a little as she tried to find the words to explain herself. I didn't know why she was so scared, we weren't the police. It wasn't until she spoke that it all made sense.

"Look, it wasn't anything malicious," Aisha said. "I needed the money. Desperately. My dad is sick, has been for years. I've been doing what I could to float the medical bills, but I was drowning. Really drowning. Then I met Leon, and he wanted to help. I let him." She sighed, her feet shuffling. "I know how it sounds, but I wasn't with him for the money. I loved the guy. Really."

I tried to sound understanding. "It must have been hard to lose him so suddenly."

"It truly was," Aisha agreed. "I don't understand it. Leon was in perfect health and I know he had that place inspected before he rented it. If there was an issue with the pipes, he would have known and had it fixed."

The side of my face burned from Joe's intent glaring. He was probably thinking what I was, that Aisha was on to something. Why would Leon's landlord rent the place out if it had issues that could cause a serious accident? It didn't add up.

I sucked in a sharp breath. "What happened to the maps, Aisha?"

"I took them."

The admission was so straightforward and quick that I almost didn't catch it. I was about to ask her to explain more, but she beat me to it.

"Like I said, Leon was helping me with Dad's hospital bills, but it wasn't enough. When the sheriff told me that Leon had died, I panicked. I knew the maps were worth some money, so I figured why not take them? I could sell them and pay off the bills until I figured out a better solution. I made a mistake."

It was hard to tell if Aisha was sorry because of what she did or because she got caught. When it came to petty crimes, this wasn't what I expected coming here. For some reason, I pictured the woman as some evil mastermind who went out of her way to rob the man she was dating, but that wasn't it, was it? Aisha was a desperate woman in an even more desperate situation. I didn't know what I would do had I been stuck between a rock and a hard place as she was. Likely not steal, but who knew?

People did things that were out of their character all the time and, in this situation, Aisha's heart was in the right place. Sort of.

I crossed my arms.

"I'm not going to stand here and judge you," I told

Aisha. "Coffee knows I've made my own mistakes in the past. But that map I mentioned, I really need it. If you give it back to me, I promise not to mention any of this to the police." *Because they're not even looking for the rest of the maps,* I added in my head.

"You'd have to ask Drake if you want your map back," Aisha said.

My stomach dropped to the floor. "Drake Jenkins? Leon's landlord? What does he have to do with this?"

The woman squared her shoulders and zipped up her hoodie tighter. "He's the one I gave them to. He was supposed to help me sell them for a good price, but the sleazy idiot stiffed me. Said Leon owed him a bunch of cash, so he was taking the maps as payment instead." She pointed to the table behind her. "That's why I'm here. I was hoping the moron sold them off for cheap and I could get my hands on them again. Try another way. But no luck."

"Not to rush anyone, but are the three of you interested in purchasing anything?" the vendor of the table we stood at asked.

My cheeks reddened, angry splotches spreading down my neck. I was so invested in Aisha and her story that it completely slipped my mind that we were in a public space. Apologizing profusely, I left Joe to sweet talk the vendor while Aisha and I stepped aside. My hand reached for her arm and I rested it there gently. "I hope you find a solution to your problem," I said. "I'm sorry about your dad."

"Thank you."

With a wave, I watched Aisha Lang slip between the tables and disappear from my sight. In the time we had been here, a few more customers came in and the market was starting to resemble the booming hub of flurried activity I remembered. People chatted over found trinkets, haggled prices, and voices fought for attention as I stood in the midst of it all. Meeting Aisha did not go as I planned, but it wasn't all for nothing. We had a new clue to follow, a thread to unravel to get us closer to the map.

Then why was there a pit in my stomach? Why did it feel like we hit another dead end?

CHAPTER 14

Harry Houdini

T he witch had ruined my life. Again. I gave the large pot blocking my entrance to my kingdom one more shove, my fur rubbing against the textured clay.

Nothing.

My teeth chattered as the delicious scent of ripe berries and plump carrots rose in the air. How dare she prevent me from entering her House of Green in such a rude manner? It was unbecoming of her. This wasn't the first time she had come up with ways to stop me from eating what was rightfully mine, and it was beginning to frustrate me to no small extent.

Maybe it was time to move on. Go somewhere where I was appreciated.

I squeezed around the side of the small house in the witch's backyard, my butt knocking over another planter. I glanced back, whiskers wiggling. Good.

Slowly, I made my way out of the garden and out of the witch's life. Another scent caught my attention and my paws buried deep into the earth stopped me. Nose in the air, I sniffed for the abysmal intrusion. The smell was familiar enough, but I couldn't quite put a paw on it. Then, it hit me.

My head swiveled around just in time. Behind me, a grayish man floated past the House of Green and towards the witch's front door. There were two similar humans behind him, except they weren't quite right. More like the obnoxious blonde hanging around the witch.

What was it she called them?

Oh, yes. Ghosts.

My eyes rounded to see clearer in the dark as the ghosts neared the house. Suddenly, two more appeared. Three more. Too many to count, even if I wasn't too tired to bother.

The ghosts paid me no mind, concentrating so hard on the witch's house they didn't realize they were being watched. Stalked. By a most expert night crea-ture. My paws padded softly, and I swung my rump to and fro, following them like the predator I was. When I realized the ghosts weren't leaving, I paused again. What did they want?

My neck stretched to see around the porch. The ghosts gathered right outside the front door, deliberating. Inside the house, the witch was clueless, as was her nature, I realized now. She was completely oblivious to the danger right outside her door. Where was that blood-smelling man she kept around? He wasn't much better, but at least he could offer her some assistance.

Eyes narrowing on the path leading into the woods, I considered my escape. I should go. The witch made it clear I wasn't welcome. Still...

I pressed closer to the house. The brick bit into my skin and I rubbed against it, eliminating an itch that had been bothering me for hours.

With a shake and shimmy, I backed up until my side hit the pipe hanging off the side of the house. I had used it many times to get in while the witch was gone. What's one more? Clipping my nails to the metal, I began my ascent. Step by step, I put more distance between me and the ghosts, the smell of their arrival getting weaker. Using my nose, I pried the upstairs window open and rolled into the farmhouse. My bottom hit the creaky floorboards with a thud.

Step one complete.

Looking around, I found the objects that would make the most noise and got to work. One by one, I tore them from their spots, knocking them into the walls, the floor, and each other. Anything to get the witch's attention.

Outside, the wind howled as the incoming snow storm got closer and closer.

My attention landed on the bedroom door and the angry footsteps running up the steps.

The witch owed me big time, and she was a fool if she thought I wouldn't collect. I shall take my payment in cookie form, thank you very much.

CHAPTER
15

The noise from upstairs was deafening. I plugged my ears in the hopes of tuning it out, but there was no point. Whether I wanted to or not, I had to put a stop to it.

Turning off the movie I was in the middle of, I reluctantly poured myself off the couch and stomped up the stairs. My steps echoed throughout the empty farmhouse as I neared the bedroom. A loud clatter made me jump and I nearly face-planted as my foot caught the landing. I growled, sparking up my magic immediately.

Harry Houdini was about to get his butt zapped for whatever commotion he was causing this time.

Lightning sparked off my fingers as I wrapped them around the bedroom door handle and twisted. Inside, the room was a mess. There were several books randomly thrown about. My clothes had been ripped off their hangers and lay in a pile on the floor, and my favorite vase lay shattered next to the nightstand. What has gotten into him?

"Harry! What now?" I screamed.

My eyes darted around the room to find the rascal. I checked under the bed, behind the large mirror in the corner, even in the clothes pile. No raccoon.

A flurry of fur and feet caught my attention. I twisted my head to the window, finding it unlocked and wide open. Since I would never leave it ajar in the middle of winter—the heating bill alone would kill me —I knew the fuzzball had to be hanging off the side of the house. Keeping my hands down so as not to startle him, I crept to the windowsill.

The first thing I noticed when I looked out was Harry's chubby behind scurrying off into the darkness. His little legs scratched against the cobblestone path leading to the greenhouse, and he swayed his rump back and forth as he put distance between himself and me.

The second thing I noticed were all the ghosts.

My heart sank, chest constricting at the sight of

them. They came out of nowhere, dozens it seemed, and were all heading in the same direction—right toward my front door.

What in the name of lattes is happening?

I pushed my head further out of the window, straining to see where the mysterious figures had come from. The night was thick with dread, the air heavy and still. It was then that my eyes caught sight of the giant rift around the back of the greenhouse. It pulsated and thrummed with an otherworldly energy, a dark glow casting eerie shadows over the backyard.

The sheer force of its presence made my knees buckle. Its energy seemed to consume everything in its vicinity, warping reality itself. Even from my vantage point, far above the ground, I could make out the dark, shifting forms within the rift, moving with unnatural speed. My father's monsters at the ready.

A shiver ran down my spine as I realized what was happening. My mouth went dry, and I swallowed hard, the fear almost paralyzing. I took a hesitant step back from the window, my heart pounding in my chest.

"Wards," I told myself. "I need wards."

I didn't know what the ghosts wanted, but considering how many of them there were and how determined they looked to get into the farmhouse, I was willing to bet it was nothing good. Another warning from father dearest, no doubt. Since there was no way for me to make it past them, I had to think on my feet. The only thing I could think of was strengthening the wards Gran had around the house. There was a chance they wouldn't work against incorporeal beings, yet what choice did I have? I had to at least try.

Rushing out of the bedroom, I reached Gran's magic room in record time. My feet skidded to a stop in front of her old supply wardrobe and I flung the doors open so hard they banged against the wall. Eyes scanning the shelves, I gathered the ingredients I needed. A sprig of rosemary, a handful of salt, three black candles, and chalk for sigil drawing.

Cramming all the supplies into a bag I found in a corner, I hightailed it out of the room and headed downstairs. By the time I got there, the energy in the house had shifted and my stomach turned, my mouth feeling like cotton candy. There was a heaviness to the place that wasn't there before. A darkness.

I gulped down air, my head tilting to the side. In the windows, I could see the crowd of ghosts inching closer to the farmhouse. They filled the porch with their otherworldly presence, but not one tried to come inside.

"What are you doing?"

A whoosh at my back made the hairs on my neck

stand straight. I turned around, breathing a sigh of relief when I realized it was only Stella. Pressing a finger to my lips, I motioned to the ghosts outside.

"Um, why?" Stella whispered.

I shrugged. Keeping my voice low, I lifted up my witchy goodies to show her. "I'm going to try putting wards up. Stay close. I don't want to push you out accidentally."

"As if you could," Stella retorted.

Despite her attitude, I noticed her creep up towards me. Satisfied that I had my familiar close, I dumped the contents for the spell on the floor and got down to business. My witch magic skills were quite pathetic, but wards were easy spells to cast, especially when you had the targets close by. If I did this correctly, I should be able to expel the ghosts away from the house. At least far enough that I could walk out the front door. When it came to negative energy, wards were as primitive as mosquito spray or a strong citronella candle.

I shivered as the weight of the creep show outside the house reached me. *Time to get to work.*

The first thing I did was to sprinkle salt at the base of the front door. I made sure to do this from a distance because getting too close to the spirits made my head pound as if a hammer were striking it. I couldn't help but wonder if Hades ever suffered migraines from being surrounded by so many dead souls. The thought seemed absurd, and I shook my head with a smile. Ancient deities didn't get headaches, surely.

Following the basic spell Gran had taught me years ago, I picked up a sprig of rosemary and began rubbing it over the door frame. I moved slowly and meticulously, ensuring that every inch of the wood was covered. The familiar, earthy scent of rosemary filled the air, reminding me of happier times than this.

Next, I lit the candles and watched them burn down.

While the candles burned steadily, I grabbed a piece of chalk and began etching out sigils on the door. My artistic abilities were limited, and the drawings came out clumsier than I would have liked. Despite my lack of skill, I focused on the intent behind each symbol, remembering Gran's words that the power of the spell lay in the belief and effort behind it. I carefully drew each line and curve, hoping that it would make up for any imperfections in my handiwork.

Finished, I stood back to inspect my work. I was no Picasso, but it would have to do.

"Maybe add a little pizzazz," Stella said from behind me.

I nodded. "Good idea."

Wiggling my fingers, I waited until they were coated

in magic to touch my palms to the runes. The energy in my body intensified, and I closed my eyes tightly, concentrating on releasing my magic into the spell. After so many hours of practicing, I had my Hades magic down pat. The energy drifted from me without a hitch and this time, I didn't even get knocked on my butt as a result.

My lips twitched into a sly grin.

"Did it work?" I asked with one eye open.

Stepping away from the door, I followed Stella to one of the bay windows, my chest rising and falling with anticipation. The fog in my brain had lifted, so I knew I managed to have an effect of some sort, but considering how many ghosts there were before, I wasn't sure what to expect. When I peered outside, my breath hitched. The spirits were still gathered in the yard but they were retreating; floating back toward the greenhouse and the rift open there. The wards were working!

"I did it! Stella, I did it!"

The ghost rolled her pale eyes skyward, unimpressed.

I checked the window again, then closed the curtains. My legs shook as the adrenaline started to wear off and I was hit in the face by what had occurred. If it wasn't for Harry Houdini, I never would have had time to protect myself. Somehow, in his own wild way, the bugger actually saved me. *Did Harry do it on purpose?*

Chuckling, I stepped away from the window. Of course not. He was probably looking for snacks.

"What was that about?" I asked Stella.

The ghost's eyes narrowed. "Power play?"

"I don't think so. If Hades wanted to show his hand, he wouldn't do it this way. What did that even accomplish?" I thought back to the rift I saw earlier. "I think he's getting ready. Mom said the Sisters are gearing up and we have less than a week left before the Blood Moon. Whatever the coven is doing, it's making the rifts stronger. Or the block between our worlds weaker. I don't know which one."

"Hate to imagine what will come through if they succeed."

I bit down the inside of my cheek because Stella was right. If this was any indication, once the Sisters open the doorway for good and Hades makes it to this side as he planned, we'd be dealing with a lot more ghosts. And who knew what else? My eyes traveled to the kitchen window and the view of the forest beyond.

"Do you think there were more of them because of the ley lines being so close?"

Stella's expression darkened as she thought about it. "It's possible. I always feel stronger here in the farmhouse. Why?"

"I'm not sure. I feel like there is a connection there, yet I can't quite put my finger on it."

"Well, you better figure it out," Stella said. "And fast."

My gaze stayed on the horizon and the dark line of trees formed a barrier between me and the unknown. Somewhere beneath the soil, the ley lines pumped magic through the town, an undercurrent of energy that could be felt in everything we touched. I used to love knowing that we lived above so much power. Now, I feared what it could mean. One thing was for certain: Stella's words could not ring any truer.

Time was not on our side.

In the last year, there had been plenty of moments where I felt that I was quite literally racing against the grains of sand falling down. But now?

I shivered.

So much was at stake that I didn't know where to start. It was the first time in my life that I had the support I needed and the magical prowess to succeed, but I had no clue how to use any of it. My mind raced, plans and ideas floating before but never touching down.

I may not know how to stop the Sisters, though that didn't mean I couldn't move forward. All I needed was to take this one step after the other, like I did with every other bizarre case I helped on in the past. Begin with the obvious and work from there.

My head turned to my familiar. With my father's threat looming over her head, Stella was running out of time with the rest of us.

I spent the rest of the evening watching the windows, waiting for my father's next move.

CHAPTER 16

The morning brought with it a glimmer of sun and a much needed change of mood. I awoke to the sound of birds chirping and the whistling of light winds outside the window. Somehow, despite last night's uninvited guests, the farmhouse felt cozier than ever.

It gave me the determination I needed to come up with a plan.

Step one, coffee.

Step two, call Joe and see if he's up for a drive.

Step three, get a hold of Drake Jenkins and shake him until he gives up Leon's map.

I tightened the band in my ponytail and turned on the coffee machine. Periodically, my attention drifted to the front door, and the sigils drawn there, but I tried hard not to let it bother me. It couldn't hurt to have more protection on the house and even though I hated the way we got here, it was nice to know that I was more than capable of performing basic spells. For once, I didn't feel like a complete failure and it was giving me all the warm fuzzies.

I filled up a giant mug and topped it off with a dollop of cream, then sat down at the kitchen counter in front of my laptop. It took me a few tries to find Drake's information. At this point I was familiar enough with the online space to get what I needed without breaking a sweat. And I only had to restart my ancient laptop twice to do it. Win-win!

Typing up a quick email, I waited to press send. My fingers hovered over the keyboard while I waited for confirmation from Joe that he was able to join me. On any other day I'd have made the trek to see Leon's landlord on my own, but last night had shaken me. Not to mention that I promised Joe I'd avoid leaping into danger without backup and I wanted to keep my word. It wasn't the worst idea to bring a vampire with me, in case Drake decided to try something funny.

The landlord didn't strike me as a violent man, though who knew these days? Look what happened to Leon.

Nothing. He died because of an accident.

Why was I having so much trouble accepting that?

My phone lit up, and I barely glanced at it before sending off the message to Drake. Keeping my fingers metaphorically and physically crossed, I downed my coffee and poured another cup, waiting. It took less than fifteen minutes for Drake to respond. As it turned out, the prospect of someone else renting the apartment above the Inky Atlas was all the bait I needed.

"Business as usual," I murmured.

Grabbing the car keys, I put on my coat and boots and slowly stepped outside. My eyes kept watch for any residual spirits lingering, but they seem to have vanished overnight. Before getting into the car, I ran to the greenhouse and peered around the side. The rift was also gone.

"Phew," I breathed out. "Finally, a lucky break."

Climbing into the Beetle, I strapped my phone into the holder on the dash and typed in the destination. It was an address I didn't recognize. I was surprised Drake suggested meeting somewhere other than the map shop. He mentioned checking up on another rental property, so I assumed that was where I was headed. Yet I didn't recall finding anything on more rentals when I looked the landlord up online.

Perhaps I wasn't as good of a sleuth as I thought.

Putting the phone on speaker, I dialed a number and peeled out of the driveway. The phone rang twice and a low, deep voice answered. "Sheriff Romero here."

"Sheriff, hello!" I exclaimed, somewhat surprised that he answered. The sheriff had been especially difficult to get a hold off lately. I started to think he was avoiding me.

"Miss Addison," he said, his voice coming out in a drawl. "How can I help you?"

I veered onto the main road and sped up. "I wanted to see if you had the chance to look up Drake Jenkins yet."

"I have," the sheriff answered. "No red flags. Not that it matters, since the Hunt case is closed."

"Right, of course. Did any other rental properties come up under his watch?" I pressed on.

The sheriff mumbled words I couldn't make out. Somewhere near to him, a dog barked. I jumped in the seat, startling. Since when did Romero have a dog? Weird.

"No rentals, no," the sheriff said. The dog barked again. "Listen, Miss Addison, I'm really sorry, but I have to go. There is some work at the station to take care of."

I bit my lip. "Oh, sure. You're at the station? I didn't realize we have a police do—"

The line went dead as the sheriff hung up on me. I stared in disbelief, my eyes blinking. *How rude.*

Driving to the destination Drake specified took longer than expected. I had veered so far from my regular haunts that I wasn't sure we were in Orchard Hollow anymore. If it weren't for the sea keeping me in constant company, I'd have been worried I was lost. As it was, I was simply venturing as far off the grid as was possible without completely falling off the face of the earth. The map on my phone froze as I turned off the main road leading through town and down a wide path lined by trees. Occasionally, a small cottage would appear out of nowhere, but for the most part, there was nothing but solitude here. The kind that made it hard for someone to hear you scream.

I checked my phone, the message from Joe letting me know he'd arrived putting me at ease. Relief flooded through me. At least I had backup.

I steered carefully, guiding the car down unfamiliar paths. Up ahead, the road split into two and I followed the directions I had memorized earlier, since my map was all but useless out here. I hoped there was more reception when we got to the property Drake led us to so I could text Cilia about the location in case things went south. Not that I thought they would. At least, not really.

"Better safe than sorry," I muttered.

Another turn brought me to an even more isolated location where the trees encroached so much on the road I felt I was slicing through them. The branches overhead formed a natural tunnel, while the underbrush threatened to swallow the narrow dirt track completely. The air grew thicker, deepened with the scent of pine and damp earth, and the occasional rustle of unseen creatures heightened my anxiety. The oppressive darkness of the forest seemed to close in, amplifying my sense of isolation and heightening the panic that gripped me.

Finally, after fifteen minutes of pure panic, the trees parted to reveal an adorable sight. The forest abruptly gave way to an open space. Before me rose a low hilltop, its gentle slopes covered in lush, green grass. The road I was on continued upward, winding its way to a tiny, charming cottage perched atop the hill. The cottage had a rustic, fairy-tale quality, with ivy climbing its stone walls and mismatched bricks laying the foundation.

At the base of the hill stood two cars, one of which I immediately recognized as Joe's. Parked beside it was another car, a sleek, modern model that seemed out of place here. The presence of these cars reassured me that I was not entirely alone in this remote location. I took a deep breath.

As picturesque as the area was, I had no reception and couldn't discern any sign of life other than the three of us. I rolled down the window to see the place better. "Who would live all the way out here?"

Parking next to Joe's truck, I climbed out and looked around. There was no sign of Joe or Drake anywhere. Worry twisted up my gut as I searched around the vehicles. Where could they have gone?

I noticed a set of boot prints on the snow-drizzled ground and followed them to a nearby barn. The small building was situated further away from the main cottage, almost on the outskirts of the property. As I neared it, I heard voices drift towards me and my muscles relaxed. A moment later, Joe's deep chuckle filled my ears. Rounding the barn, I didn't gauge the slippery ground and my boots slid across, my hands reaching out to grab the side of the building. I shrieked moments before my butt hit the cold ground with an angry thud.

"Piper! Are you all right?" Joe yelled out, already at my side and helping get back on my feet.

I scrambled up, using him like a tree trunk to climb on. When I was finally upright and my cheeks stopped burning, I said, "All good."

"Sorry to drag you out here," Drake said. He walked toward me, extending a leather gloved hand. His long tresses were tied in a fashionable man-bun and he wore a thick jacket, indicating he was planning to be outside for some time. "The woman who rents this place needed some work done, and this was the only day this week she would be out of the house."

"No problem. We won't keep you long," I said.

Shaking my hand, the landlord walked to the end of the barn and picked up a toolbox, placing it on top of a small cart filled with pipes. He wheeled the packed thing over a few feet, then collected some more items to add to the pile. By the time he was done, the cart resembled a circus car with a mountain of objects balancing awkwardly atop it.

Drake stood back to inspect his work. "You mentioned renting out Leon's old place?" he asked. "I should let you know it won't be available until next month. I'm having the building inspector check everything to make sure there are no more issues after what happened."

Joe's eyes landed on me. On any other day, I'd have continued the charade, pretended to be interested in the apartment above the Inky Atlas, and coerced answers out of Drake to the best of my abilities. But I was tired. The long drive sucked the energy right out of me and if I was honest, I didn't want to spend too much time out here in the middle of nowhere with a man who quite possibly could have stolen and sold the one thing I needed to save not only myself but also him. Drake didn't know it, of course, but humans were in as much danger as us paranormals with Hades on the prowl to take control of Earth.

I glanced at Joe again with a look that said, "Let's get this over with."

"We know about the maps," I blurted out.

Drake's hand dropped away from the cart. "What maps?"

"The ones that are missing from Leon's shop," Joe explained. "The maps that Aisha stole and gave to you to sell for her."

The landlord's unease could be sensed from miles away. His body grew rigid. I watched him take a few clumsy steps backward, his back knocking into the barn wall. His hands shot up defensively. "I don't know what you're talking about."

"Let's cut the lies," I said in return. "We don't care about any of it, but there is one map that I need and I'd appreciate it if you could hand it over."

The next two things happened so fast I barely had time to register them. One second I'm staring at Drake sweating nervously in front of me and the next he is running toward his car so fast there's a blur left behind him. I turned on my heels to chase him, but luckily, Joe was one step ahead of me and Drake. His vamp speed kicked in and he zoomed past me to catch up to Drake. His large hands wrapped around the man's jacket and he yanked him back, slamming his back against the barn wall again.

"Like Piper said," Joe growled out, "we only need one map. Then we're out of here."

Drake's voice came out in a tremble. "I-I don't have them," he stuttered. "I sold them to some guy online. He paid in cash, and he paid fast. No questions asked."

At this, Joe's grip tightened.

"I swear I'm telling the truth!" Drake whined. *I hate this guy.* "Why do you care about them, anyway?"

"That's none of your business," I said. "Do you think you can track the buyer down?"

Joe's hands tightened further. "Consider this your motivation."

Pressed between Joe and the wall, the landlord looked like a rag-doll. His legs buckled and he all but dangled as Joe held him up. He opened his mouth and somehow, I could tell I wasn't going to like what he had to say.

"I'm sorry, I can't," Drake mumbled. "It was an anonymous sale. As I said, no questions asked." He glanced around Joe and me toward the small cottage on the hill. "Look, those maps were on my property, so I didn't do anything illegal here. Now, if you don't mind, I really need to get these repairs done before

Miss Cooke returns. I can't afford to lose another tenant."

Reluctantly, Joe loosened his grip and let Drake fall back to the ground. The landlord brushed himself off before grabbing the stacked cart to wheel it away from us and to the cottage. As he passed me, his words echoed in my head. The blood drained from my body, a memory flashing before me.

I reached for Drake, grabbing his sleeve to stop him in his tracks. "Did you say Cooke?" I asked.

"That's right," Drake replied. "Sasha Cooke. The renter of this lovely establishment."

His lips moved as he continued to speak, but his words did not reach me. I stood there, dumbfounded, staring at the cottage in the distance. My mouth gaped and shivers tripped down my spine. I knew that name.

My teeth knocked together.

This was very bad news.

CHAPTER 17

A branch slapped me across the face and I yelped as I ducked out of the way of a second one coming in strong. My feet were tangled in roots and mud and I was pretty certain the leaves brushing up against my leg were poison ivy. At my back, Joe waited patiently, not at all bothered by the wildness of the hiding spot I crammed us into hours ago.

"A Sister of the River, huh?" he mused.

I peeled apart two tree branches to watch the cottage from afar. My brain was working overtime to make sense of the situation we found ourselves in. Sasha Cooke. The name sounded familiar the instant I heard it. It took me a second to put the pieces together and remember the conversation I had with my mother, but once I did, there was no going back.

Sasha Cooke was a Sister, and we were standing right in her backyard. I looked around. Well, hiding in the forest behind her backyard was more like it.

As soon as I realized who the witch renting Drake's cottage was, I hightailed it out of there with Joe in tow. We had to get away before Sasha returned home. I wasn't planning on staying away, though. Making Joe follow my car, I turned us off a fork in the road I saw on my way in and we parked in an out of sight lot that didn't appear to be used by anyone in years. From there, I made Joe hike through the forest to a spot we could watch the cottage from but not be seen.

It would have been a brilliant plan if not for the weather. My toes were basically frost-bitten in my boots and there were icicles forming on the tip of my nose. To make things worse, Sasha hadn't come back yet, and the sun was starting to set.

"We should head home if she's not back soon," I said.

"It could very well be a coincidence."

I arched a brow at Joe, letting go of the branch I was holding. It hit me in the neck and I winced at the sharp slice of pain on my skin. "What are the chances that a Sister of the River lives right here in our town at the same time that Leon is found dead?" I asked. "This is no coincidence."

"What are you thinking happened?"

Checking on the cottage, I frowned when there was no movement inside or a car pulling in. I'd assume Sasha would need a vehicle to get in and out of the place. Unless The Sisters had some other magical way to get around the rest of us didn't know about. Somehow, I highly doubted that.

Shifting my weight from one foot to the other, I ignored the needles running up and down my calves from standing too long in one place. "I think I was right to question how Leon died before. It may have been gas poisoning, but I don't think it was accidental." I glanced at the cottage once more. "I think Sasha is here to keep the map secret. I believe with almost complete certainty that the Sisters are tying up loose ends and Leon and his maps happened to be one of them."

I expected Joe to tell me how insane my theory sounded or to try to convince me to leave. Instead, he did the exact opposite. My boyfriend simply blew on his freezing hands, widened his stance, and kept watch.

"Then we wait," he said.

Warmth bubbled up inside my chest. I reached for

Joe's hand and wrapped my fingers around it. "You're the best, you know that?"

Joe chuckled.

As he turned his attention to the cottage, another idea popped into my head.

"We could wait or..." I nudged my head toward the off beaten road leading up to the cottage's backyard. Since the location was so isolated, there was no need for a fence or any sort of external security. Anyone could walk right in. My lips tapered off into a sly grin. "Since she's not home, we could scope the place out."

Again, I expected some form of a rebuttal, but was met with only a head shake and Joe's defeated grunt. He straightened out, reaching so high that his head brushed against the tallest of branches. Keeping his eyes narrowed on the target, he parted the trees to give us space to sneak out. I followed quietly, keeping one eye on the road running behind the cottage in case a car came by.

Joe noticed me moving skittishly and laughed. "I'll hear it if she comes. Don't worry."

Right. Vamp hearing.

The words added some courage to the situation and a pep to my step. I skipped up the rocky path with Joe at my heels, reaching the perimeter of the cottage's backyard in record speed. There were what appeared to be the remnants of an old fence on the ground, and I had to hop over the wood planks to avoid tripping. It was shocking I didn't land on my butt. Perhaps I was getting stealthier in my old age.

When I landed on the other side of the planks, I paused. There was a faint light in one of the rooms in the house. For a second, I thought Drake was here, but that couldn't be right; we saw him leave over an hour ago.

I pointed to the light. "Do you think she's home?"

"Doubtful," Joe replied. "It's probably on all the time."

The light from inside helped me see a little better, though with the sun setting fast, it was getting darker by the minute. A golden glow spilled out from the windows, slightly illuminating the backyard. I rubbed my eyes, trying to focus them in the dimming light as I navigated my way around the random piles of wood and overgrown bushes that had overtaken the rear of the cottage.

As quaint and picturesque as the place appeared from the front—with its charming shutters, blooming flower beds, and neatly trimmed lawn—it was the exact opposite back here. The yard resembled a jungle from the Jurassic era, wild and untamed, with towering weeds and creeping vines that seemed intent on reclaiming the space. Fallen branches and rotting logs littered the ground, creating an obstacle course fit for a horror movie.

I worried I'd break my neck before we even had the chance to reach the house. With every step, I felt for solid ground in the undergrowth. The air was thick with the scent of earth and the overgrown bushes brushed against my legs, their leaves damp with dew.

Staying true to my character, my foot caught on an object lying on the ground and I stumbled forward. My arms shot out in front of me as I shielded my face from the fall. In a flash, Joe was pulling me back before I broke my nose slamming into the ground.

Heart racing, I pressed my back into his chest, my knees knocking together.

"Close call," I breathed out.

When Joe didn't answer, I turned to look at him. His gaze was on the ground, a foot away from where I tripped. Irises wide and dark, he had the look of someone who had seen a ghost. I should know, I was well acquainted with said look. Turning back around slowly, I followed the trajectory of his vision.

My breath fell out of me in a sharp gasp.

Laying on the ground before us with skin so blue it matched the Orchard Hollow sea was a woman in her late fifties. There was a large piece of broken fence off to the side of her, the very thing I must have knocked over when I tripped. In my fall, I seem to have exhumed the woman from the place she lay hidden. Her long hair spilled out around her head, golden with streaks of gray throughout. On her neck, a silver chain hung, twisted so tightly it cut into her skin. The woman's hands were in fists at her side and she had a look of absolute horror etched on her face.

I opened my mouth to scream, but no sound came out. The woman was dead. There was no mistaking it.

Trying again, I collected myself and asked, "Do you think that's—"

"Sasha Cooke."

It wasn't Joe that interrupted me. My body stilled, legs so taught they could snap. Swiveling around, I turned on my heels to face the forest only to see a shadow-cast figure enter the backyard. Hips swaying, the figure sauntered toward us with the steps of a fox, all cunning and sneaky.

My eyes widened in disbelief.

"Mom?"

CHAPTER 18

"Hi, honey. Surprise!"

A strong wind blasted at me, carrying my hair away with it. The unruly strands twirled atop my head and clung to my lips, sticking to the lip gloss I put on earlier like socks to a heated dryer. I peeled away a few strands, my eyes so wide my forehead hurt from the exertion.

Was it me or did it get colder all of a sudden?

I looked at the woman standing before me. "What are you doing here?"

Mom rose on her tippy toes to look behind us at the body on the ground. Eyes dark and gloomy, she rolled back on her heels and clicked her tongue. Her hair, the same wild red mess as mine, fell over her shoulders, limned in the golden glow streaming from the cottage window.

"Same thing as you, I wager," she said. "I found out there was a Sister in the area and came to check it out. Noticed your car by the turn off, so I figured you beat me to it." She wrinkled her nose. "You should be more careful where you park, darling. Anyone can see your man's beast of a car from a mile away."

My eyes flicked to Joe, who shrugged and rubbed the rear of his neck. Stepping aside to reveal more of Sasha Cooke, I said, "We have bigger problems than Joe's truck right now. Your Sister is dead."

"Killed, I take it?" my mother asked.

"Looks to be," Joe answered. "Welcome back, by the way. Good to have you home, Sylvie."

Sauntering our way, my mother pointed a long slender finger and ran it across Joe's chest. My boyfriend's brow raised in amusement as she puckered her lips his way, her hip cocking.

She smiled like a fox ogling her prey. "Good to be back, handsome."

I felt my lunch come back up my esophagus. Which only reminded me of how hungry I was, which made me more nauseous, which... I collected myself. Why was I spiraling right now? Oh, yes. The dead witch at my feet. I bristled. Turned toward the body and took a tentative step forward.

"What happened to her?"

My mother shrugged, her hands clasped tightly together. "Magic. Obviously."

"What do you mean?"

"It's in the air, honey," she exclaimed. "Can't you feel it? The entire place stinks of it."

Tilting my chin up, I sniffed the air, realizing too late how ridiculous I was being. What did I think would happen? That I would physically smell the magic? Foolishness. My mother was a stronger witch than me, the most powerful one I'd ever met after Gran. It stood to reason she would sense energies I couldn't. Especially since she'd spent years of her life with a coven that practiced dark magic. If there was evil energy here, Mom would know it.

I toyed with the idea of asking her to explain, but left it alone. Now was not the time, and this was definitely not the place.

"We should leave. I'll call the sheriff on the way out and let him know what happened. He is not going to be happy."

Turning to me, my mother winked, placing a hand on my shoulder. "Let me handle Romero. You two head on out. I'm going to see if I can trace anything else around here that might help us."

She was talking about the map, of course. I started to object, but thought better of it. My body was shaking from the cold and wetness had penetrated my boots, making my toes feel like icicles in my socks. I desperately needed a hot shower and a cup of coffee. Perhaps simultaneously.

After suggesting Joe and I help her clear the area in case whoever hurt Sasha was still around, we proceeded to check for intruders. It didn't take all that long, considering that Joe did the bulk of the work while Mom and I stood to the side and poked around the body. Satisfied, she waved us off and waited until we were stomping down the hill to start whatever it was she had planned. As we walked, I continued to look over my shoulder at the cottage.

Our only lead was dead and no matter what Mom thought, I knew she wouldn't find anything at the cottage. Unease clawed its way up my spine.

Why did my mother return? It couldn't have been because of Sasha. At least, not only because of her. I knew Mom long enough to know when she was keeping secrets and that woman was up to no good.

Something told me I'd need a stronger drink when we got home to the farmhouse to handle the rest of the evening.

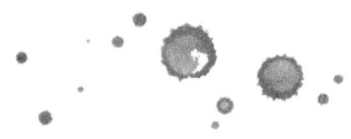

"More wine, honey?"

True to form, my mother dangled a bottle of Shiraz by the neck in front of me. I shrugged off the knitted throw draped over my shoulders and reached out with an empty glass. More wine was an under-statement. While it was lovely having Mom back—for the most part—it was the other woman that returned with her that was causing me grief.

No, that wasn't quite right. Isabella Beaumont's ghost wasn't the problem. My gaze peeled away from the wine and landed on the living room corner where my familiar stood scowling.

If looks could kill Stella Rutherford would have murdered the vampire had she not been dead already. The women had not spoken a word to each other since Mom returned from the cottage with Isabella in tow, and I doubted it would change any time soon. I was developing a migraine from all the tension in the room. It didn't help that I was the only one who could see the spirits and thus the only one lucky enough to have to endure their childish behavior.

"Knock it off," I hissed out.

"Knock what off, darling?" Mom asked.

I shook my head and gulped down my wine, the acidity helping clear my head a little. "Not you," I explained. "We have a ghost standoff on our hands. I don't know what their problem is, and no one is telling me anything."

Across from me, settled in the plush cushions of the living room armchair, my mother cackled, downing the remainder of her wine in one go. She glanced over her shoulder, her eyes landing past Isabella's four-inch heels. "Leave them to it," Mom said. "We have things to discuss."

It was nearly impossible to tear my eyes off the women. Isabella was already fierce when she was alive, but being dead made it even more difficult not to notice. The ghost's long hair fell down her back in perfect, smooth waves. The power suit she died in didn't have a wrinkle in sight, and it was next to impossible to get past the overall sense of confidence she exuded. Then there was Stella, who filled the room with her presence to the point of suffocation. Between the two of them, it was a surprise I was able to concentrate on anything else.

On the plus side, having Isabella around seemed to be the only thing that made my familiar quiet and I was partly grateful for the reprieve from her snide remarks.

You won some, you lost some.

I shot Stella a serious glare and said, "Don't think you're off the hook. Once we're done here, you two better come clean about your weirdness."

No answer. *Wow.*

"All right, your turn," I said, turning to my mother. "Care to explain why you're really back?"

"I told you, honey. For Sasha."

A throat cleared in the kitchen as Joe fixed himself a vampire drink. He walked toward us, glass in hand, filled with a deep red liquid that I chose to think of as a Bloody Mary. Despite knowing that Joe didn't drink human blood, seeing it put me on edge, a quirk I knew I should work on soon if we continued to get more serious.

My boyfriend put the cup on the side table and sat down on the couch next to me. "Any thoughts on who may have killed the witch?"

"No! Absolutely not!" I interrupted. My hand shot up in argument and my face burned, my nerves finally unraveling. "We are not playing this game anymore. People are dying and our time is running out. Leon Hunt didn't die of a gas leak. I don't know how I know it but I do. And now with Sasha killed... She was a Sister for coffee's sake! It is all connected." I flicked my eyes to my mother. "As is your return. Now spill it."

An uncomfortable silence spanned between us. It swallowed up the air in the room and made me sink into the couch, swallowed entirely by velvet and dense feathers. My hand shook as I waited for Mom to speak up. In my grip, the wine sloshed around and I briefly glanced at it to make sure I wasn't spilling anything. Intimidation only worked if you weren't a hot mess express train heading straight for a rock wall.

Out of the corner of my eye, I noticed Stella's ears perked as she registered my sudden bravery. Much like at the sea with Nancy Steeles, a darkness took over me and I couldn't help but snap. Perhaps it was all the anxiety bubbling up to the surface or, as Stella suggested, my father's angry blood coursing through me. Whatever caused it, I was glad I spoke up.

Mom was not getting away with secrets this time.

"Piper…" Joe whispered in warning.

My mother cut him off. "No, she's right," she finally uttered. *I knew it!* Mom's face grew ashen and though she tried to act nonchalant, I noticed the discomfort immediately. "I did come back because I figured out that Sasha was staying in Orchard Hollow, though it isn't the only reason I'm here."

"This has to do with Joe, doesn't it?" I asked. "It's why you've been so squirrelly about it every time I asked. What's going on, Mom?"

To say my mother was wishing to vanish right at that moment would be an understatement. Her cheeks sucked in and her head twisted from side to side as she scanned the room. If we were going through airport security, the woman would raise enough red flags to get us detained for days. Now, sitting here in my living room, her old living room, she only looked afraid. And small. I had never seen my mother this way.

She reached into her purse resting at the foot of the armchair and pulled out a silver vial. Proceeding to slide it across the coffee table toward me, she waited until I had it in my hand to breathe out.

"What's this?" I asked at the same time that Joe said, "Sylvie, you didn't."

"I'm sorry, handsome," my mother said. "It had to be done."

My blood pressure spiked, heart racing in my chest. "What am I missing here?"

From her corner of the room, Isabella whispered, "This is going to be bad."

I battled the urge to scream at everyone to stay quiet until Mom explained. Sensing my restless nerves, my mother smiled in a way that only she knows how and I immediately relaxed.

"I paid a visit to Joe's family," she said.

And we're back in panic mode. My eyebrows arched so high they brushed against my hairline. "Mom! Why? You could have been killed." Wincing at my choice of words, I turned to Joe. "Sorry."

"No, no. You're quite right," he agreed. "My family could have torn you to pieces. Why Sylvie?"

Mom nudged her pointed nose to the vial in my hands. "We both know why. Your lot is one of the original vampire families, Joe. Their blood is potent. We need the lineage for the spell to seal the gates to work."

I swallowed, horrified. *Ew. Please, don't let this be what I think it is.*

"Yes, that is vampire blood you're holding," Isabella said. "Probably from a lot of them."

The vial fell from my hands as my fingers snapped open. Joe jumped across the couch, catching it right before it shattered. I bit down on my tongue, then met my mother's solemn gaze. "You asked for their blood? Seriously, Mom. That is morbid."

"Maybe so, but it's the only way." She nudged a thumb in the general direction of Isabella. "That one gave me the idea, actually. Vampire blood is a strong conduit. Most blood is, but vamps are stronger. And to have the blood of an original family will help us close the rifts to the Underworld." She paused briefly. "For good, honey. We can put an end to this forever."

I rubbed the bridge of my nose until it hurt. "This is why you wouldn't tell me anything about Joe's part in your plan. You knew he'd want to stop you from going to his family's coven. That he would warn you against it."

"Still think it was a foolish play, by the way," Joe muttered.

Mom brushed us both off. "Foolish as it was, I did what had to be done. I cut a deal with your family, Joe.

They help save the world and I won't breathe a word of their location to anyone, so don't even ask me for it. I know you have your werewolf friend looking."

"How do you—"

"Joe, please. I'm not as flighty as I seem." She turned her thunderous gaze on me. "Now all we need is Joe's contribution and we're set."

The way she said it made it appear so simple. So easy. Yet it was none of those things. My mother may have found a way to seal the gates and stop Hades from crossing over, but we didn't know where the ritual would take place and call me careful; I wasn't going to start celebrating until we had all the pieces of the puzzle in place.

Out of the corner of my eyes, I saw a flash, followed by Stella's blonde hair being flipped from one shoulder to the other. The ghost grimaced. "Too bad that vamp blood can't tell you where to look."

For once, I completely agreed with my familiar.

CHAPTER 19

The sound of humming and whistling filled the farmhouse. I stepped out of the shower to follow the tune that made the place reminiscent of a kids' movie. I half expected to find animals and animated crockery cleaning the place when I got downstairs, though, knowing my luck, it would only be Harry Houdini stealing snacks again. Instead of either scenario, I found my mother swinging her hips to the song she was singing while frying eggs. Her hair hung loose at her back and she'd switched out the bell-bottoms she wore yesterday for a loose maxi-dress in sunflower yellow.

The song picked up the beat and my mother's hips followed.

I chuckled. "Good morning."

"Hi, honey," Mom cooed. She pointed to the pan on the stove. "Omelet?"

Not having the heart to tell her that what she was making was definitely not an omelet, I only smiled and said, "Coffee for now. You want one?"

"Already on my second. It's been a heck of a morning."

I was about to ask her what had her up in knots today when the quietness in the kitchen made me realize we were entirely alone. As in, not a ghost in sight. The kind of alone I hadn't been in a while. I jerked my head around, straining my neck to inspect the lower level of the house. "Hmm. Strange."

"What's that, darling?"

"Stella and Isabella are nowhere to be seen. Usually Stella is all up in my business about what I'm wearing at this time of day." I pointed to my mismatched socks and bright pants. "It's her favorite way to start the morning."

At the stove, Mom flicked her wrist, and the pan jumped. Eggs flew everywhere, coating the once sparkling countertop in greasy stains. "Check outside."

I followed her instructions and walked to the front of the house. Peeling back the curtains, I scanned the front yard, finding it empty. Cramming my hands into a knee-length cardigan, I walked to the front door and unlocked it, poking my head outside. Standing on either side of the porch were the two ghosts. Their eyes narrowed on each other and their arms folded across their chests in parallel. From here, they looked like two cats in a standoff, which, I supposed, was not too far off from the truth.

I shoved my head out further. "You two need to figure out your differences!" I shouted at them. "You're adults. Act like it! We have a world to save and no time for your melodrama."

With that, I slammed the door and stomped back to the kitchen. I was pretty certain that the ghosts were telling me off behind my back, but I didn't care. If they weren't going to share their issues with the group, I had no patience left for the childish feud.

When I got to the kitchen, Mom was no longer at the stove but was setting up my laptop on the island. She fiddled with the wires and I cringed when I saw one land in her mushy salad. Mom used the back of her dress to wipe it off and plugged the machine in. *Coffee help me.*

"What are you doing?" I asked.

My mother smiled mischievously. Her fingers danced on the keyboard and she kept one eye on me and one on the screen. I watched her use her free hand

A.N. SAGE

to stab the eggs with a fork, chewing loudly. On the screen, a virtual call website opened up, the other side dark.

Mom held up a finger. "Give her a second to connect."

"Her?"

The screen flickered as the second line of the video call came to life. Mom shooed me off with her hand, pointing to the chair opposite the island. "You can listen, but stay out of sight."

Since the coffee machine was well out of view of the laptop, I had no choice but to obey. Walking away with my tail between my legs, I scurried to get a mug, trying not to clink the spoon on the glass as I stirred in the milk. On the laptop, I heard a rustle followed by the sound of a chair scraping on the floor.

"Sylvie? Can you hear me all right?" a vibrant voice asked.

I itched to creep closer to Mom to see who it belonged to.

My mother tilted the screen away more in a final attempt to tell me who truly ran the show around here. "Maisie! Hi!" she cooed into the screen. "I can hear you fine. Good to see you again."

Reaching for a piece of scrap paper and a pen, Mom scribbled down a name and passed it over to me on the island counter. I snatched it up hungrily, reading over the swirly script of her handwriting. Maisie Fletcher. Sister of the River, lower rank. Had it out with Sasha last year.

I turned the paper around, searching for more, but that was all she wrote. Disappointed, I grabbed my cup and settled across from Mom at the counter, making sure I wasn't getting in the way of the camera. I hadn't realized that she was calling a Sister. It was no wonder she wanted me out of sight; the coven had no idea that I even existed. The last two witches who found out were no longer around and I doubted Mom wished to out her Hades spawn over a video call.

"Why the sudden call?" Maisie asked. "I thought you were off handling your mom's estate?"

My brows hiked up. Seeing the shock on my face, Mom bristled, but didn't explain. Not that she could at the moment. I figured she had to give the Sisters some excuse for why she was leaving the coven so close to the ritual, but I didn't know she used Gran's death for it. Especially considering that Gran died over a year ago. Another thing I bet the coven didn't know.

Mom cracked her knuckles and faked a frown. "I'm still here. It's all so sudden and tragic, but someone has to get the house ready to sell," she lied. The little sneak. "I'm afraid I'm not calling with good news."

"Oh? What's happened? Is this about...you know?"

"No, something else," Mom replied. "Geez, I don't quite know how to say this. Sasha is dead."

My heart stopped, waiting to hear the woman's reply. The silence that followed was agonizing, and I bit the tips of my nails in anticipation. Finally, Maisie let out a long, dwindling sigh and asked, "Sasha Cooke?"

"Yes," Mom answered. "I'm sorry to have to be the one to break the news. I know you two used to be friends before the fiasco last year. I figured you'd want to hear what happened."

"Of course. Thank you for telling me. It's—" Maisie sucked in a trembling breath "—shocking, truly. How did it happen?"

Across the table, my mom stretched out her hands and her eyes briefly flashed to me before returning to the screen. "I don't have all the details yet, but as soon as I find out, I'll let you know. Have you talked to Sasha lately?"

"Me?" Maisie asked, baffled. "You must be kidding. I haven't spoken to her since she tried to steal my place in the head circle, then disappeared off the face of the earth. Come to think of it, we should let the other Sisters know. They can stop looking for her now."

Taking another piece of paper, Mom scribbled a second note and slyly tossed it my way. I caught it before it flitted off the counter in a clumsy attempt. My eyes ran over the words. Sasha escaped the coven. No one leaves easily. Sisters were mad. Have been looking for her since.

Oh, my.

It appeared that the Sisters of the River weren't all as devoted as I believed. Mom had never mentioned anyone running off on the coven, certainly not someone who was living in our own town. Then again, perhaps she didn't know. I made a mental list of all the things I needed to ask her when she got off the phone. It was a very long list.

My head throbbed as I thought about the new information. If Sasha was hiding from the coven, why would she kill Leon to help them? The puzzle I thought I was starting to figure out crumbled before me as more questions arose than I had answers for. What was going on here? *Darn it!* I hated going one step forward, only to be pushed two steps back. It seemed to be a pattern of mine lately, and it infuriated me to no small extent.

Breathing in deeply, I worked to keep myself from getting worked up and focused on Mom and Maisie instead.

"You should tell the head witches," Mom

suggested. "I'm not sure when I'll be done here, but you're right, they should know to stop looking."

"One less deserter to worry about," Maisie said.

My mom cringed visibly. As did I.

How many others ran away from the coven? I wondered.

It was clear Maisie saw my mother's reaction because she corrected herself immediately. "I'm sorry, that came out wrong. It's terrible she's gone, really," she said. "Me and Sasha may have not gotten along, but I never wished her harm. Don't tell the girls, but I always hoped she was happy wherever she was."

"You haven't talked to her at all?" Mom pressed.

Another slow sigh rose from the laptop. "I'm afraid not. I'm sure Sasha knew that I'd tell the Sisters if I heard from her," the witch said. "It was a shame to lose so many years of friendship. What can you do, right?"

"Nothing now, I suppose."

"Oh, my!" Maisie exclaimed suddenly.

The high pitch of her tone made both me and my mother jump in unison. My arm swung around, knocking into the half-empty coffee cup beside me and pushing it off the counter. I jumped to catch it, but I was too late; coffee was everywhere.

I looked up at my mom, an apology stretching across my features. Thinking fast, she covered the commotion with a cough. I prayed Maisie didn't catch on.

"You know who you need to call, don't you?" the witch asked, completely oblivious. Thank the latte gods. "Lya. Lya Delacruz."

Across from me, Mom wrote the name down and underlined it twice. "Why Lya?"

"Didn't you know? Rumor is that she was the one who helped Sasha make a clean break," Maisie replied. "Nothing was ever confirmed, still, we all knew it was true. They were tight as thieves for as long as I knew Sasha. I'm sure she'd want to know her friend died."

I heard my mother ask Maisie for contact information right before sneakily find out that she was with the coven preparing for the ritual for the last two weeks. It wasn't much, though it did tell us that Maisie was nowhere near Orchard Hollow when Sasha was killed. And considering that Mom was certain magic was used, that left us with only one viable suspect.

Whoever Lya Delacruz was, she was about to get a visit she didn't expect.

I pushed away from the island and poured a second cup of coffee while Mom wrapped up her call. Leaving her in the kitchen, I marched to the front door, taking my caffeinated life juice with me. There was one more thing I had to handle before moving forward, and I couldn't wait to get it settled.

Swinging open the front door, I let the wind envelop me as I stepped onto the porch where the two ghosts stood in silent confrontation. It was time to put their weird feud to end once and for all.

CHAPTER
20

S heriff Romero leaned against the side of the police cruiser parked in my driveway. His hat sat low on his head, the brim obscuring half his face from view. Even without seeing his eyes, I could tell he wore his usual expression. Neutral with a hint of frustration.

I closed the door behind me and cleared the space between us, my heart jumping in my chest with every step. Glancing behind me, I nodded at Stella Rutherford. The ghost stayed behind as soon as the sheriff pulled up, though I was pretty certain not being near Isabella had a lot to do with that choice. It took an hour of dealing with their negative behavior to finally get to the bottom of what was bothering the women, and when I did; I worked hard not to laugh. Turned out it was a giant misunderstanding.

Back when both were alive, Stella's husband booked a room at the Rose Hollow Hotel; one that Stella assumed was because he was cheating. Having previously seen her husband being too chummy with Isabella, she made up a story in her head of the two going behind her back and never let it go. Stella was similar to our resident raccoon that way—once she got her mind on something, she latched her teeth into it.

The funny part of the story was that Arthur, Stella's husband, reserved the room to surprise her with for their upcoming anniversary. A room Isabella, as the previous owner of the hotel, was helping him get ready for the big day. Of course, Stella died before the plan came into fruition, but not before she decided that she was not a fan of the vampire. When Isabella died, it made her rage kick to the surface.

For my own amusement, I chose to think that jealousy had a bit to do with it, too. Not being the only ghost in my life that I could actually speak to pushed Stella over the edge. At least, that was what I told myself.

Behind me, my familiar raised two thumbs up and urged me forward. She stayed glued to the porch with an invisible force, refusing to budge. Knowing Stella, it would be some time until she came to terms with how wrong she was.

I loved every second of it.

Skipping over a fallen tree branch, I came to stand in front of Romero. "Hi, Sheriff," I said, my smile hiding my discomfort. "What can I do for you?"

"Three days," Romero replied.

I scratched the back of my head, the motion loosening the braid I put in that morning and making my hair look like a bird's nest in the rear. "Pardon me?"

Romero stretched his arms wide, then rapped his knuckles against the car's hood. The signature hat he wore tipped backward and, for the first time, I saw his gaze land on me. Black circles lined his tired eyes and even though I knew it was impossible, I was sure he had gained more wrinkles since the last time I saw him. Whatever was happening, it gave the sheriff a run for his money.

"The recent deaths in Orchard Hollow have drawn in a crowd," he said solemnly. "Not the kind we wished for. Last week, I got a call from an old friend at the bureau to give me a heads up and now with the death of your witch, there is no stopping them."

"I'm sorry sheriff, I don't follow."

Romero's eyes narrowed, the creases around them

deepening. "The bureau is here, in town," he said. "At the station. They arrived on Monday and have been a huge thorn in my side since. They even brought trained dogs with them, Miss Addison. A good handful of them."

Ah. That explains the barking.

"I thought I could hold them off, turn them around somehow, but I'm afraid that is not an option."

"What does that mean, exactly?"

The sheriff's lips down-turned. "You have three days to do what you need to do, Miss Addison," he said. "After that, the bureau is officially taking over the open cases and I can guarantee that they will watch our town like hawks. Better start spreading the word to the other paranormals. If you've got magic, now is the time to hide."

Lowering his hat again, the sheriff gave me a curt nod and climbed into the car. The ignition sparked to life, and the sound made goose bumps crawl over my arms and legs. As though we weren't in a tight spot already, now we had to race against the clock while simultaneously avoiding the cops. Wonderful. The patrol car pulled out, then stopped. I watched Romero roll down the window halfway to peer out of it.

"I'll do what I can to steer them out of your way," the sheriff said.

I smiled, waving goodbye. "Thank you."

As I watched the car speed away, my entire being folded in on itself. My knees knocked together, and it took me a few moments to collect myself again. As if we didn't have it hard enough. I wasn't sure why this was the case, but it seemed that whenever I caught a break, the rug was yanked out from under me. Life was constantly finding a way to throw me off track.

And now this.

A low whistle snapped me out of my head. I turned toward Stella, her plump lips forming an O as she waited for me on the porch. "Don't be glum, Piper," the ghost said. "It isn't your color."

She turned on her heel and floated to the door, beckoning me to follow.

"Didn't you hear what he said?" I yelled after her. "Three days and we're done."

The ghost flashed a tight-lipped smile.

"You've dealt with worse."

She vanished. In the window, I saw her reappear as she made her way deeper into the house where my mother and Isabella waited. Shaking off the remnants of self-pity, I climbed the porch steps and stifled whatever doubt lingered inside my chest. My fingers lit up with magic and I reached for the handle, the need to find a solution settling deep in my belly.

"We need to find Lya Delacruz," I called out to my mother in the kitchen. "And we need to do it fast."

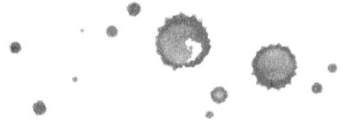

Fast was an understatement when it came to Sylvie Addison. I didn't even finish speaking before Mom had people on the phone and twenty tabs open on my laptop. For someone who had been hiding off the grid for the last two plus decades, she sure had a way with online research. Somehow, without breaking a sweat, Mom found out Lya's phone number, tracked her to a motel on the outskirts of town, and pinged her private social media profile to a coffee shop near there.

All before lunchtime.

I stood back, baffled at her superior sleuthing expertise. "You are scarily good at this."

"Thank you, honey," my mother said. "I did spend years undercover with a dark magic coven. It paid to know my way around the internet."

She wrote down the address of the motel and closed the laptop, pushing away from the table. Tossing an apple from a bowl into her purse, she brushed past me, saying, "If we leave now, we can be there by two."

I started to speak, but she stopped me before I could utter a word.

"Joe is meeting us there. Don't worry."

"How did you..." I paused. "Never mind. I do not want to know why my mother and my boyfriend have exchanged numbers. Let's go."

Mom winked. "That's my girl. I call shotgun!"

"Mom, you're literally the only other person in the car."

Walking out the door, she shrugged and skipped down the driveway toward the Beetle. Her long coat dragged across the snow and she left a trail behind her that darkly reminded me of a body being dragged. Mom stopped to wait for me by the front door, looking around. "Honey, these days, who knows how many spirits I have to fight for the front seat? Now hurry. I'm freezing."

Speeding up, I unlocked the car, and we poured ourselves in, waiting for the heat to kick in before I started driving. We drove in silence except for the sound of the blinker on turns and the few times Mom turned on the radio, found nothing that appealed to her, and turned it off again. It was nice to have this comfortable stretch of quiet between us. Mostly because we both needed it to prepare for what came next.

Somehow, I felt Lya was the answer. Call it

wishful thinking and yet, my body sensed the urgency that thrummed beneath all the nerves and dread. Another Sister close to Orchard Hollow so close to the Blood Moon could not be a coincidence.

Or perhaps I was only praying it wasn't.

The Lucky Thirteen Motel sign poked its head on the horizon and both Mom and I sat up a little straighter. My fingers white knuckled the wheel as I pulled us into the small parking lot where Joe already waited. He must have sped all the way here. As we climbed out, I gave him a quick peck on the cheek and avoided my mother's inappropriate comments.

"What's the plan?" I asked them.

"I was thinking Joe could distract the manager while the two of us scope it out."

I looked between her and Joe. "Sounds good to me. If there's anything to worry about, I'll text you."

"All right," Joe agreed, holding my hand. "If you see Lya, stay away. We don't know if she's dangerous, and I'd rather not have to worry about you two."

"Aye, captain," Mom teased.

She gave him a mocking salute, then yanked me out of his hold and dragged me behind her across the lot. With an apologetic shoulder shrug, I followed the wild woman as she took us around the building to a set of stairs leading to a second floor. As Mom started her ascent, I checked behind us, worry starting to rise within me with each step taking us further up. Joe's words replayed in my head. We really didn't know if Lya killed Sasha. It seemed unlikely considering that she was the one who got her out of the coven, though.

My boots landed on the top landing and a long stretch of hallway emerged before me.

"This way," Mom said.

She pointed to the right, and I stretched out to see further down the corridor. To our left, a low railing lined the passage while room doors stood stacked on the right. For the most part, Lucky Thirteen was a normal motel, aside from being almost entirely abandoned.

"Did you notice we were the only cars in the lot?" I asked.

Mom nodded. "Not a popular place by any means," she said. "Do you think Lya is in the room?"

"It's possible she didn't drive." My nose scrunched as a thought occurred to me. "Hey, how do you know which one is her room, anyway?"

"I have my ways. Come on, it's this way."

Since I did not wish to find out what her ways entailed, I locked my lips tightly shut and pitter pattered after her. Moving like a jungle cat, Mom maneuvered past the doors so quietly, I started to wonder if she cast a silencing spell prior to us getting here. I, on the other hand, trampled behind her with the sound akin to a herd of elephants running from danger.

To say we were opposites in every way was an understatement.

Mom came to an abrupt stop, and I rammed into her from behind. Her hair fell into my open mouth and I spit it out, gagging a little. Oblivious to the fact that I ate half her head, she spun around and said, "This is it."

Up ahead, a door similar to all the others we passed stood tall. We crept toward it, keeping our backs against the wall and our steps light. When we reached it, Mom made a random motion with her hands I didn't understand and swung around the single window facing the hallway. Her body moved in a flash as she passed by the window, peering inside.

A frown creases her forehead. "It's empty."

"As in she's stepped out?"

"As in she checked out," Mom corrected. "It looks cleaned out."

Reaching into her purse, she pulled out a plastic card and what looked to be a set of hairpins on a key loop. Ducking beneath the door handle, she wiggled the items around, her fingers twisting and turning and her face marked in concentration. A few seconds later, a click sounded inside the lock mechanism and Mom opened the motel room door.

My jaw hit the ground.

Seeing my face, Mom grinned proudly. "I'll teach you later."

Checking once more for anyone else around, we slipped into the dark, empty room. My hip bumped against a chair near the door, and I grunted, closing the door behind me quickly. I rubbed the sore side. Pulling out my phone, I turned on the flashlight and waved it around the room.

As expected, it was completely abandoned.

The bed was perfectly made, corners tucked with a towel shaped like a swan sitting on the comforter. There was the distinct smell of disinfectant in the air, telling me it had been recently cleaned. Clearing the main area that housed the bed, two side tables, and a medium-sized television, I walked to the bathroom. Much like the remainder of the room, it was sparkling. There were tiny shampoo and lotion bottles stacked on the sink counter and several bleach-white towels sitting on the ledge of the bathtub.

If Lya was here before, we'd never know it.

"We got our killer," Mom announced from outside the bathroom door.

Come again?

I burst into the main space and came to a stop mere inches from her. My eyes widened at the salt circle on the floor with my mother smack dab in its center. She blew out the sage stick she held and tossed it into her bag. I glared at her. "How can you possibly know that?"

"Same magic," Mom replied. "I traced it with a locator and it's spot on. The magic that was used to kill Sasha was all over this place."

I helped her disembark the circle and dusted off any remaining salt on the ground. Together, we checked the room from top to bottom, making sure we didn't miss anything that might point us to a ground-breaking clue. Having found nothing for our troubles, we were about to leave when my gaze caught on a loose floorboard beneath the bed. I dropped down and ran my fingers across it. My skin grazed a scrap of paper and I pulled it out from the place it got caught in the wood. Motioning for Mom to come closer, I brought the torn paper up.

"What is it?" she asked.

I turned the paper around, noting the few numbers on the edge. It appeared to be a corner of a larger sheet, one that I recognized right away. This looked an awful lot like the maps I saw in Leon's shop before.

Twisting the paper to face me, I clicked my tongue, sucking in a sharp breath. "How much do you want to bet this was the map we were looking for?"

"You have a theory, don't you?" Mom asked.

I closed my eyes and let my jumbled thoughts pour out. "What if Sasha was the anonymous buyer Drake mentioned? If she was running from the coven, it stands to reason she wouldn't be on the same page as them as far as the whole end of the world thing goes. It's possible she knew Leon had the map and tracked it down after he died. Was killed for it, likely."

"And Lya was the one to do it," Mom added. "It would make sense since the coven has been so secretive. If they thought one of their own was working against them, they would send someone to handle it. Especially this close to the big day."

"You really think Lya would kill her own friend for the Sisters?"

Mom's eyes grew dark and stormy. "You would be shocked to know what those witches were willing to do."

"Good thing they didn't suspect you," I whispered, my chest heavy and my throat full. Eyes darting around the room, I stood up, pulling Mom up to join me. "Let's get out of here. The place is giving me the creeps."

Walking behind me, Mom locked up the room after we left and we speed-walked back to the car. Once we were settled in the safety of the Beetle, I told Joe to finish up and to meet us as Bean Me Up. What we needed was coffee and a place to regroup. I couldn't think of a better spot than the cafe.

It was my only real solitude since Hades found a way to make me feel unsafe, even in the confines of my own home. I seriously could not wait for this entire mess to be over with. Provided we all lived to see the day.

CHAPTER
21

W e piled into the back office of Bean Me Up, filling it up until it was so crammed it was hard to breathe. Between my mother, Joe, Cilia, and the two ghosts, it was a full house. Outside the doors, Rory manned the cafe while the rest of us got to work, researching every angle to help get us closer to the ritual location.

Knowing, or somewhat knowing, who killed Sasha and Leon did not help move the needle forward in that part of the dilemma we faced. Not to mention I still had nothing to show Romero for my efforts, so as far as I knew, the bureau was not leaving town anytime soon. Our best bet was to get as many eyes as we could on as much information as we could gather, then deduce from there. The plan was to use every piece of myth written on Hades to narrow down places where the Sisters might strike. That, in combination with the three numbers I was able to pull from the torn map piece we found in the hotel, gave us a jumping off point.

It wasn't much, but it was a start.

"I have Iceland as a possibility," Joe announced, highlighting a section of a book he had opened before him. "Anyone else have that?"

We all checked our respective tomes and open browsers. As part of his contribution to our valiant team, Joe wheeled over dozens of books from his shop and even drove into a neighboring town to purchase several more. I supplied the coffee, Mom kept us fed with snacks from the convenience store down the street, and Cilia let us borrow three laptops from the hotel. Then there were the two ghosts, but they mostly watched, occasionally adding their opinions when they weren't too busy scowling at each other.

I rolled my eyes as Stella stuck her tongue out at Isabella's back. "No Iceland for me," I told the group. "I read mentions of Australia, but it wasn't concrete."

"It's probably nothing," Joe mumbled, moving on to the next book in his tall stack.

A knock on the office door made us stop reading. I turned around in the office chair to see Rory poke her head through the opening. The teen smiled warmly, dangling a bag of fresh muffins in my face. "The baked delivery came in. Anyone hungry?"

My stomach chose that exact moment to growl so loud it echoed down the entirety of the cafe. Cheeks red, I got up and walked to Rory, grabbing the bag from her hands with my head down. The others didn't appear as enthused as me to be eating. For a brief second, I identified with Harry Houdini.

"Good thing the raccoon isn't here," Stella said, reading my mind. "You might have competition for those artery cloggers."

Ignoring her, I tore off a muffin top and shoved it in my mouth, making sure to chew extra loud for Stella's benefit. Polishing off one muffin, I took a few sips of London Fog Latte and started on the next book. As I opened the page, a commotion in the alley behind the cafe made me stop. Everyone turned to the door leading there.

My head swiveled to Stella, then to Joe. "I bet you that's Harry. He probably smelled the muffins all the way at the farmhouse."

Willing my magic to rise, I wiggled my fingers, the blue sparks dancing across my skin. The energy of the electricity was so familiar and so much my own that I realized I missed using magic. With the warning from Romero hanging heavily over me, I had been extra careful not to bring it out, but right now, all I wanted was a little taste of the power I harnessed. And, if I was honest, I needed a break from the research. My head pounded, and we still had nothing to show for all the time we put in so far.

"I'll see what the furball is doing," I said, pushing the door open.

Walking out into the alley, I expected to see Harry knee deep in some sort of trouble. That raccoon was always causing havoc, and judging by the sound we heard earlier, he was probably knocking over garbage bins in search of his next meal. What I didn't think I would see as the door slammed behind me and pushed me further into the alley was the gargantuan rift slicing the air in half.

I came to a full stop. Head cocking to the side, I inspected the rift, my mind working overtime to understand why it was here. There were no spirits in sight, which should have been a relief, but instead was causing me nothing but worry. What did it mean? Why was it here?

I had too many questions.

"This can't be good," Stella said next to me.

Shivers ran up and down my arms. "What are you doing out here?"

"Came to see what all the commotion was about," Stella answered. "And I want to watch you zippity zap the beast. This is not what I thought I'd find."

"You and me both," I admitted. My focus drifted from my familiar to the rift ten feet away. "You should head back inside. To be on the safe side."

With a nod, Stella started to vanish. Her body grew more and more transparent as she disappeared, and I waited for her to be gone before inspecting the rift and hopefully closing it. Except it never happened. Instead of leaving, Stella did the exact opposite. Her ghostly body stayed frozen in place, not a limb moving.

"What are you doing? Go!"

My urgent pleas fell away into nothing. I watched in horror as my familiar's eyes widened, her mouth straining to speak. Her gaze dragged to me before landing back on the rift. It was then that I understood.

Leaving her side momentarily, I marched toward the opening. My pulse raced and my legs pumped as I slammed my feet into the pavement. When I reached the rift, I was shaking from all the pent up anger inside me.

"Let her go!" I screamed into the dark void. "Now!"

A low growl made the muffin I ate earlier start to

climb back up. "You don't make demands, daughter," Hades hissed.

The dark slice in the air rippled, and I felt it push me backward. My feet slid on the ground, my balance weakening. Shooting my arms out, I grabbed onto the side of a dumpster to right myself before I dropped down. Inside the rift, my father laughed.

I didn't know how much one could despise a parent they longed for until that very moment.

"What do you want?" I hissed.

"To have your word," Hades answered. "That you will surrender."

I grit my teeth together. Silent.

"I see you need more convincing," my father bellowed. "So be it."

Everything that came next happened so fast it almost spun in unison. The rift rippled again, and a black line of magic shot out from within. Inside its core, I saw the same blue streaks of electricity I was used to wielding. The rope-like energy zoomed past me and headed straight for Stella Rutherford. It wrapped around her, squeezing her in the same manner as a python squeezes a hare before swallowing it whole. Stella's eyes bulged as her ghostly form was dragged into the rift.

"No!" I screamed. "Stop!"

Hades didn't. Obviously.

Horrified, I watched as my familiar was pulled closer and closer to the rift until she was a mere foot from it. Her gaze flashed to me and my chest twisted at the fear behind her eyes. I threw my arms toward the rift, blasting the energy my father commanded with my own magic.

The dark thread holding Stella didn't even flinch.

My tongue swelled in my mouth, the realization of what was about to happen dawning on me. I couldn't lose her. Stella wasn't only a familiar. She was my best friend; my family. Feet sliding on the slippery pavement, I struggled to stand. If I had to throw myself in with her, so be it.

As I clawed my way to the rift, another flash of movement zoomed past my periphery. All I recognized was glossy dark hair and heels higher than the tallest tower in King City.

Isabella.

The vampire ghost reached Stella before I could. She growled deep in her throat as she used her arms to slash against Hades's magic. For a few brief moments, nothing happened. Then, the grip he had on Stella weakened. If only for a flash. It was all the time Isabella needed.

She reached for my familiar, yanking her out of the darkness and throwing her in the opposite direction. Stella flew. While she was airborne, the vampire ghost met my widening glare.

"End it, Piper," she said.

I didn't have time to scream before her spirit was sucked into the void of the rift. My eyes burned, tears blurring my vision. I tried to stand, but my legs gave way and I fell down with a thud. Isabella was gone. My father took her.

I couldn't believe what had happened.

"Piper! Get down!"

Joe's voice snapped me back to the moment, and I didn't bother to turn to look at him before dropping to the ground. My body coated the pavement from head to toe, a pancake in the shape of Piper. Coming in hot from behind me, Joe slid into view until he was right in front of the rift. His palm shot to the side and I watched in awe as he flipped a kitchen knife from the cafe in his free hand. Without a second thought, Joe sliced the knife across the fleshy cushion of his palm. I averted my gaze, unable to see Joe's blood.

By the time I looked back, Joe had already dripped a few droplets into the rift.

The black void holding my father and Isabella captive shook violently. A screeching sound emanated from within and I had to press my hands to my ears to keep from shrieking with it. Inside the rift, my father roared. My eyes grew large as orbs as the rift sealed shut before me.

In a rush, Joe ran toward me and kneeled at my side. "Are you all right?"

"Me?" I shook my head. "Your hand."

"I'll heal." He looked over his shoulder. "I guess we know your mom was right about my blood being a deterrent."

I scoffed. "Thank you. I wish I didn't come out here. Isabella...she's—"

"She saved me," Stella whispered.

Spinning around, I jumped up and rushed to her. Stella wasn't a hugger and it wasn't that I could embrace her anyway, but all I wanted was to wrap my arms around the ghost and squeeze the daylights out of her. A smile tugged at my lips, my teary eyes crinkling. "I'm so glad you're safe."

"Why did she do that?"

My spine grew rigid. I caught my familiar's attention, my features softening. "I guess she was done fighting with you."

While Stella continued to stare blankly at the spot where the rift was only moments ago, I inspected Joe's cut. It wasn't as deep as I imagined and, thanks to his vamp abilities, had already started to heal. I ripped off my scarf and tied it around the closing wound until we could get him patched up inside. Then I waited for

Stella to snap out of her daze so we could go inside where the others waited. It all happened so fast they were still gathering items for retaliation spells by the time we stepped through the open doorway.

My mother body-checked me into a bear hug and held me so tight my eyes popped. I shimmied out of her vice grip, saying, "I'm fine. But Isabella." I bit my bottom lip. "She didn't make it. He took her, Mom."

"We'll get her back," my mother announced. "I don't know how, but we'll try. Sit down. Have a coffee. You need a second to decompress."

I sat opposite Stella, watching her like a hawk. The ghost was the quietest I'd ever seen her, and I wondered if she was in some sort of shock. Or a stupor that she wouldn't be able to snap out of. Outside the office, the clamor of customers brought some peace to my shaky thoughts. Stella was safe. Most of us were. For now.

But for how long?

A steaming cup of coffee slipped into my hand. I took a sip, my muscles relaxing. Thanking Mom, I reached to put the mug on the desk, pushing aside a stack of books to make space. A bright red cover peeked out from the pile and I reached for it, the image somehow familiar. I tilted my head to look at the sparkling red stones of the cover more clearly.

"What's this?" I asked no one in particular.

"Rubies," Cilia answered. "Apparently Hades was a big fan. Some say he built the Underworld from the energy harnessed from thousands of raw rubies. All hearsay, I'm sure."

My lungs forgot how to work. Eyes meeting Stella's, I unlocked my tight jaw. A single breath tumbled out of me as I breathed out, "I think I know where the ritual will take place."

CHAPTER 22

"The old mines. That has to be it."

I flipped the pages of the book from Cilia's stack aimlessly as the wheels continued to spin in my head. How did we not see this before? The caves that housed the abandoned mines were right there in front of us, and it never occurred to me. Granted, I knew nothing of the connection between Hades and the rubies until today. The information made me realize how little we knew of the danger we faced and I tried not to think about what that could mean for our imminent future.

Placing the book down, I looked up at everyone. "I knew the location would be somewhere close to the ley lines. For this to be the place where Hades's stones were once mined is too much of a coincidence. It must be it. I can feel it."

"It does make sense," my mother agreed. "Also explains why the Sisters cut me off so abruptly. They know I'm from Orchard Hollow and if they are in fact planning to summon my ex-lover in my hometown, it would stand to reason they'd keep it to themselves."

I groaned. "Ew. Mom. No more referring to Hades as your lover, please."

"Ex, honey. I would never bed the man again," she corrected. Then, under her breath added, "No matter how great he was."

Bile rose in my throat. *If only I had the power to reverse time and un-hear that.* I looked at my lame, magicless fingers. *Stupid Underworld magic.*

It took all of me to shove past the mental imagery and concentrate on what truly mattered. My heart skipped a beat. We had it! I was so giddy I almost missed Stella's remark.

"How do you plan on getting into the mines?" the ghost asked. "They've been blocked off for decades."

"That's a good point."

"What is?" Cilia asked.

Leaning back in the chair, I took a few sips of the now cold coffee in my cup. Adrenaline carved up my spine from what happened in the alley, and I found it hard to sit in one spot. Flashes of Isabella being sucked into the rift danced before me. I closed my eyes tightly, willing the images away. Beside me, Stella pressed her lips together in a tight line, her thoughts likely on the same memory as mine.

"Stella asked how we plan on getting inside," I finally uttered. "All the entrances to the mines have been closed off for years, ever since they stopped operating."

Near me, Joe sighed. "There is also the matter of collapse. If we go in, it could be dangerous. The mines are not stable."

"Who is these days, handsome?" my mother joked.

Muttering under her breath, she left my side for the first time since I got in from the alley and walked to the supply shelf on the farthest wall. Rooting around it, Mom pulled out her purse—which she was storing in between the paper towels for some strange reason—and dug out her cellphone. Continuing to mumble incoherently, she typed something out on the screen, her fingers moving swiftly. When she finished, she tossed the phone back in the bag and the bag behind the paper towels.

Rubbing nonexistent sweat from her forehead, she looked back at the rest of us. "I can get us in."

"Who did you message?" I asked, truthfully intrigued.

"A friend that owes me a favor," Mom replied.

"Your Gran wasn't the only one with connections in this town."

"That's great, but that doesn't solve the main problem we're facing," I said.

Every eye in the room turned to me. It was so quiet that I could hear the front door lock turning as Rory closed up for the night. Their expectant glares made me quickly see that no one really thought this through. We were about to face one of the most powerful, most vicious witch covens in all of existence. And with what army? A vampire, two witches, and the child of an ancient deity who couldn't even stop a ghost from vanishing.

We were in over our heads.

I swallowed the giant lump in my throat, saying, "The Sisters of the River are not going to stop their plans simply because we crash the party."

In the cafe, the door opened again, the little bell over it ringing off the hook. I checked the gold vintage watch Gran left me, my eyes narrowing. Who was here at this hour? I distinctly heard Rory close down, and I doubted the teen wished to be here longer than she had to be. Since we took over her magic practice arena, she'd likely be more than eager to leave.

Then who was here?

"That's for me," Cilia said, jumping up. The witch

ran to the office entrance, pausing to look back at me. "You should come too."

I looked around the room, but it seemed everyone was as out of the loop as me. Joe and my mother hung back as I trailed with Cilia to the front of the building and into the cafe. I felt a light whoosh as Stella appeared at my side, staying quiet but present. My steps faltered when we reached the cafe and Cilia stepped aside.

Jaw hitting the floor, I stared at the group of women filling the space, my eyes landing on their leader. "Nancy Steeles?"

"I'm not any happier than you are," the coven leader hissed out. "Let's get this over with."

My gaze rolled over the cafe and the witches filling it. Every member of our local coven was here. I spotted a few familiar faces of women I had known since childhood and some that were new to town. No matter how long they had been around, each one showed up. What was most impressive was they weren't running for the hills. What was even more shocking was that Nancy Steeles was being polite for once.

The witch checked her watch and tapped it rapidly.

Well, as polite as Nancy could be.

I peeled my eyes off the women to look at Cilia. "You called them?"

"Of course I did," my friend replied. "Did you think I'd let you go up against the Sisters alone? This is Orchard Hollow, Addison. We help each other in these parts." Her eyes snapped to Nancy. "Some might even say we're a family of sorts."

The coven leader rolled her eyes and turned to a smaller group of women gathered by the espresso machine. Every few seconds, she peered out through her lash extensions to summon more witches into the huddle. I caught pieces of encouraging words from her as she reassured her coven members that all will be fine. It was a side of Nancy I hadn't seen before; one that was motherly and caring.

I nudged my head toward the group, looking at Cilia. "Is she really all right with helping me?"

"One thing you should know about Nancy is she might talk a big game, but when push comes to shove, she has your back. Nancy cares about this town. She won't let another coven threaten their safety."

"The Sisters are powerful," I said. "Strong and large in numbers."

Cilia chuckled, her bob bouncing around. "They don't know Nancy Steeles."

My lips split into a smile. She had a very solid point.

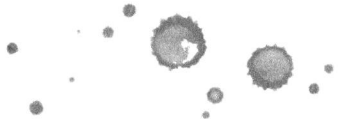

The cliffs rose around us and blacked out the sky as we marched down the less traveled path between them leading to the old mines. There were no tracks of people who had come before, the grass long overgrown to hide any clear passage that might have been here years ago. I let Mom take the lead, hanging back to keep an eye out for intruders. Our feet padded softly so as not to alert anyone who may have been close by. Especially not the Sisters if my guess was correct, and we were in the right location.

I looked down at the line of bodies before me.

We made for an odd bunch.

A vampire, a dozen witches, two warlocks Nancy roped into helping, one Hades baby, and a sulking ghost. There was a bar joke in there, I was certain of it.

We crested a large hill, the climb leaving my legs aching and breath ragged. The view from the top was breathtaking. Stretching out before us was an expansive, wild coastline. The sea clashed with the sand far below, each wave crashing with a force that sent a reverberation through the air. Above, the moon hung low in the sky, its light reflecting on the white caps of the waves like a beacon.

My heart gave a sudden jolt.

The moon wasn't just any moon. It was the Blood Moon, a rare event where the moon took on a deep crimson hue. Tonight's solar alignment, usually regarded with positive energy for witches and most other paranormals, represented a time of rest, rejuvenation, and enhanced magical abilities. The Blood Moon's energy was said to cleanse and empower; a thing to celebrate.

But as I stood there, with the considerable drop at our backs, I felt uneasy. Today, the Blood Moon meant nothing but trouble. Its red glow seemed ominous rather than comforting. The air felt charged. It was heavy, oppressive, and filled with a tension that set my nerves on edge.

I could feel it in my bones, a warning that tonight was different.

Grunting, I skirted around a group of witches to get to the front where the chained up mine entrance awaited us.

I stared at the lock that appeared to be a thousand years old with the amount of rust covering it. Grabbing a chain link, I gave it a good shake. The sound echoed through the cliffs, bounding off the rock and back to us.

"Now what?"

The jingle jangle of keys sounded behind me. I

twirled on my feet to see my mother part the crowd, an ancient keyring in her hands and a wicked grin on her face. She strolled past me with a cock of the hip and unlocked the chains in one swift twist of the key. The lock fell to the ground with a thud. The chain followed suit.

My neck heated.

"Where did you get those?" I asked.

"Ray Clifford," she said. "His family has owned the land the mines cut through since the first werewolf settled in Orchard Hollow who also happened to be Ray's great-great-grandfather."

Surprise washed over me. "Ray is a werewolf?"

Mom nodded.

"You know, I always thought that. He has a thing about him."

I pictured the ice cream shop owner down the street from my cafe and warmth filled my chest. Having known Ray since I was a little girl, the pieces started to come together. All the times he knew I was in the shop even with his back turned to the door, his quick reflexes when a kid dropped an ice cream, the way he watched you like he was tracking your every move. It was so clear he was a paranormal and I couldn't help but be relieved that he was on our side and apparently owed Mom a favor.

I didn't want to know for what, considering my

mother's past came with warning signs, so I let that part go.

Turning around to face the deep, dark entrance to the mines, a shiver tripped down my spine. I searched inside the tunnel for any sign of life, but none came. If the Sisters were here, they were deep enough that we wouldn't be able to see them from out here. As expected, we had to move inward. I looked behind me at the people gathered there. Their brave faces reflected the red glow of the eclipsed moon, making them look like a fierce army and not the people I had known almost my entire life.

Forcing my shoulders back, I stood straighter and nodded to Stella, who joined me at my side. Her pinkie twitched, slicing through my skin. My hand cooled at her ghostly touch and I felt a little less afraid with her near. My eyes settled on the tunnel ahead.

Here we go.

CHAPTER
23

The mines were pretty much exactly what I thought they would be—damp, dark, and dreary. As we made our way down the tunnels, all I could think of was if the walls were to collapse on us, no one would even know we were here. Mom assured me that Ray would call for a rescue mission, but that did little to calm my nerves. My fingers grazed the sharp, wet edges of the surrounding stone.

There wouldn't be anything left of us to rescue.

Keeping my negativity to myself, I trudged down the tunnel. The footsteps of my friends followed behind me and while they should have reassured me more, all I could think of was how much danger we might be in. It was a double-edged sword. On the one hand, I wished to be here alone so no one else could risk being hurt and on the other, if I was, I wouldn't last a second against the Sisters.

Images of Hades using me as a puppet for his wretched means flashed before my eyes. I shuddered.

No, thank you.

"Which way?" Joe asked.

I shook my wayward thoughts away to look at the fork in the tunnels we stood in. Twisting my neck to check for my familiar, I asked, "Stella?"

The ghost vanished briefly, reappearing in the entrance to the right.

"This way," she said. "The other one is a dead end."

Following her direction, we led the group to the right, steering clear of the broken machinery and rusty tools left behind. Under our feet, the remnants of an old steel track crumpled with each step, a true testament to how much time the mines have been abandoned. I tripped on a random boot and Joe caught me before I sliced my cheek open on a broken pipe. Twice.

Who left their shoes behind? Geez.

The tunnel opened up ahead and for the first time since we entered, I felt like I could take a full breath. I sucked in stale air, sputtering as dust coated my throat. "The main digging area shouldn't be too far now."

With further assistance from the werewolf ice cream shop owner, Mom was able to secure not only the keys, but a map of the tunnels from back when they were operational. There were several pockets located all throughout the cliffs on the southernmost part of town, but only one main area where the workers spent the majority of their digging hours. According to Ray, this was the place that had the largest ruby donations. Which meant it was also where the ritual would take place, permitting I wasn't leading us on a wild goose chase.

In the distance, I thought I saw a glimmer of light dance across the cave wall. Streaks of water running down sparkled like diamonds as the yellow glow flitted by. It was gone in a blink.

I stopped in my tracks, throwing my hand out to pause Joe who walked beside me. At our backs, Mom hushed the other members of the group. We all stood still as stone, waiting.

"I thought I saw something," I whispered between clenched teeth. My shaking finger pointed into the tunnel. "Right up there."

"I'll check it out."

Stella's words hung in the air as the ghost disappeared. I counted down the minutes until her return, biting the inside of my cheek the entire time. When the ghost finally manifested before me, my mouth tasted of iron and saliva.

My familiar pressed her index finger to her lips. "There's a hard left turn about thirty feet ahead," she said. "After that, X marks the spot."

"The Sisters are here?"

I didn't mean to sound so shocked, but I couldn't believe I was right for once. Relief flooded my body, only to be replaced by an agonizing wave of anxiety immediately after. I turned around, motioned in the general direction Stella pointed out, and asked, "Is everyone ready?"

Most of them agreed, but I heard Nancy bite out a snide remark about not having me in charge. For someone who supposedly had my back, she sure had daggers ready to stab into it. Ignoring her cutting words, I took the hand Joe offered and walked further into the dark.

As we crept closer to our final destination, voices began to rise in the air. Whispers and hushed tones, all rambling in a repetitive beat. Chanting, I realized. The Sisters had already begun.

I sped up, dragging Joe with me while trying to stay quiet. It was a task that didn't come easy since I was pretty sure the phrase bull in a china shop was written specifically for me. After two times of knocking my shoulder into protruding boulders and yelping, I gave up being inconspicuous and focused on being quick instead.

We reached the turn Stella mentioned, and I slowed down, gesturing for the others to get ready as we approached the digging grounds. In the tunnel, more and more items began to take shape. Hammers and hand-held drills came into view. Hard hats with names etched on them crudely with paint. I stepped over a broken oil lamp, looked back at Mom.

"What's the plan?"

She smiled, her teeth glimmering in the low light streaming from further up where the Sisters continued to chant. "The coven can distract the Sisters while you, Joe, and me focus on the doorway," she said, loud enough for everyone to hear. "If the warlocks can stay near the exit and act as backup we should have enough time to do the spell and close it up before things get out of hand."

"Stay safe, everyone," I whispered.

Not wasting more time, I ducked low to the ground and crept toward the rising sound of the chanting. The atmosphere had shifted drastically the closer we got and the light emanating from within the mouth of the caves cast deep, gnarly shadows on the jagged walls. My knees hurt from being in such an awkward position, but it was better to stay down until we could peer at what we had to deal with. One thing Stella taught me from all the times she scared the coffee beans out of me was that the element of surprise never failed in an attack.

There was a small opening several feet in front of us where the light got brighter. I slowed my stride, the others matching my pace. One by one, we entered into what was surely a Hell mouth.

My skin grew clammy and cold as we emerged on the other side of the opening. All around, spread out in the largest circle I had ever seen cast, were hundreds of candles. Between them, large piles of rubies sparkled in the glimmering light of the fire, a red glow pouring from within. I noticed a few sigils carved into the rubies closest to my feet and frowned.

No wonder we couldn't figure out the ritual details. This was unlike anything I had ever seen.

One look back at Mom confirmed she was as baffled as I was.

Gathered around the circle and holding hands were at least a dozen Sisters. They wore long, red cloaks, and their hair flowed down the fronts of the silk in smooth tresses. Though their eyes were shielded by the fabric, I knew they were closed. Otherwise, they would have seen us approach. The energy of dark magic filled the cavernous space. It coated every inch of it and made me gag.

I pressed a hand to my mouth. *What is that smell?*

A few light coughs sounded behind me as the others came into the space and smelled the same thing I was. *Is that blood?* Terror raced through me as my eyes further adjusted to the light and I could see clearer ahead.

Standing in the center of the circle were three more Sisters. Each one had a palm extended and red liquid dripped from deep gashes in their skin. It oozed into the ground, coating the object lying at their feet.

I let go of Joe's hand to step closer. My knees knocked, head spinning instantly. Lying on the floor with arms and legs extended was the body of a man. His eyes were closed, dark curls of hair gathered at the base of his broad shoulders. Surrounding the man like a crime scene chalk line were hundreds of ruby stones. Their shimmer reflected on the man's skin and I could see it ripple slightly, as though he was coming in and out of focus. Beneath the man was a whirlpool of blue light.

A breath escaped my parted lips.

This was no mere mortal.

My head turned to my mother, whose wild expression matched my own. The Sisters did it. We were too late. The doorway to the Underworld had been opened and Hades, the deity of death was out. He may not have been in his full corporeal form, but that was only because he was waiting for it to arrive. In the crowd, a single figure moved to raise the hood from her eyes. My pulse raced. I knew that face, recognized her right away. That was Lya Delacruz smiling at me with a knowing expression. No, not knowing. Satisfied.

Bile twisted in my stomach as another realization dawned on me.

"He knew I'd figure it out," I said to no one in particular. "Leon, Sasha, the map. It was all a ploy. He knew we'd follow the trail that would lead us straight here. It was how he made sure I'd be present."

An elbow nudged me, my mother trying to get my attention. I followed her terrified gaze to the center of the circle again, my soul almost leaving my body.

Hades was no longer down. He was very much awake, and he was looking right at me.

CHAPTER 24

The blue light under Hades's feet expanded further and further. Around it, the three Sisters backed up, giving it ample room to grow. Something dark and grimy reached out, but it was pulled back in by the force of the open doorway between our world and my father's. Wind circled overhead and pushed our bodies around. At the perimeter of the circle, the Sisters held their hands in tighter grips, their knuckles white from the strain. Some of their cloaks fell off to reveal ordinary women. Witches but also mothers, cousins, friends. I couldn't believe anyone would go along with this ridiculous ploy to help my father. Especially not women who looked like normal people one would see every day.

"He's not strong enough in this form!" I shouted to the others. "If we can push him back inside the doorway, we might still have a shot!"

We did not have a shot.

As soon as the words spilled out of my mouth, Hades trained his cloudy eyes on me and bellowed a deafening scream. It blasted toward me, the strength of it pushing me back. I grabbed hold of Joe, refusing to let him go. From behind me, Nancy and Cilia led the coven into the chaos unfurling inside the cave. One by one, they used whatever magic they had in their arsenal to stop the Sisters from continuing their chant. Potions and spells flew everywhere.

Some catapulted off the walls and shot back at us, making me duck periodically to avoid taking a hit. Some met their target with a quiet explosion. The witches used numbing spells, fire spells, silencing potions, whatever they could think of on the spot.

When those didn't work, they took a more physical approach.

Around us, the walls of the mining caves shook violently as the doorway bringing Hades and his monsters into our world continued to grow. My eyes widened, watching my mother pull potions from her purse to throw inside the rift. Each one had very minimal effect on closing it up.

The warlocks kept their distance as Mom

suggested at first, but seeing how little we were accomplishing, joined in quickly. I could already see their shoulders sag as the effects of using too much of their magic without replenishment took hold. At this rate, we'd be lucky to survive the next ten minutes, let alone save the world. No matter what we tried, the doorway stayed open.

In its center, my father's mocking grin grew as well. He raised a muscled arm, a crooked finger beckoning me toward him.

My teeth clenched tightly together. *I don't think so, buddy.*

"Piper, watch out!" Stella shouted.

I spun on my heels just in time to see Lya barreling toward me, a potion bottle in her hand. She raised her arm, ready to douse me in the nasty liquid that would surely cause a lot of damage. Before she could follow through, I called for my magic and blasted her with enough electricity to light up a small building.

The witch's body hurdled away from me and she smashed into the rough cave wall, sliding down to the ground. Her eyes rolled into the back of her head as she slowly lost consciousness. I stood over her, my heart racing wildly. "I have more bite than Leon and Sasha."

"T-they shouldn't have crossed us," Lya stuttered.

Fire burned in my gut. "Are you kidding? They were innocent. You killed your own friend and a guy who literally had nothing to do with any of this."

"He figured it out," Lya said, her words slurring. "Sasha told him. They wanted to—" she paused to take a breath. "—to warn you. We couldn't let that happen."

Acid rose in my throat. If I had any regrets about hurting this woman before, they were all gone now. To kill two people was one thing, I'd seen people do worse, but to justify it with so little remorse... Lya Delacruz was the worst of the worst. I raised my hand, my magic sparking between my fingers. "Stay down or I'll finish what I started," I warned the witch.

I didn't know who I was kidding because a second later, it was me flying across the cave. I vaguely heard Stella screaming again before my head slammed into a rock. Black dots swirled in my line of sight, my eyes hot and blurry from incoming tears. The inside of my brain felt like a ball was rolling from side to side and no matter how hard I worked to focus my eyes, everything swam around me.

A thousand vices gripped my arms, yanking me forward. My feet dragged on the ground and kicked up loose stones. I blinked. Once. Twice. For a brief moment, my eyes focused, and I nearly retched at the sight. Black ropes stretched from the doorway to me, electricity coursing through them. I felt its sharp zaps over and over, weakening me further. Hades was using his magic to bring me to him like he did with Stella in the alley.

His vessel was coming home.

My throat tightened, and I opened my mouth to scream, but no sound came out. I tried again with the same result. The more of my energy that Hades consumed as he pulled me to him, the less I was able to speak. A thought flashed before me.

Was this why I couldn't hear the ghosts? Was he using them the same way he was using me right now? My lungs constricted. Those poor spirits. They never stood a chance against the absolute monster that was my father.

I fought against his grip, but every movement sent blinding pains down my arms and I stopped, hanging limply as he carried me toward him. Sweat beaded on my brow and my back was so wet I was surprised I didn't slip right out of the magic ropes holding me. I wiggled my fingers. A slight tingle of the energy I harnessed zapped my skin, yet I couldn't use it to do anything of value.

I was entirely trapped.

Figures.

"Piper!" Joe screamed from somewhere in the cave. "Hold on!"

I attempted to look around, though with my current predicament, the motion was too limited to be helpful. "Find Mom!" I yelled back, hoping he heard me. "Get to the doorway!"

Right at that moment, the pull of the magical ropes pulling me intensified, and I was dragged with so much speed, my neck almost snapped. In fact, I was certain I heard a crack I'd pay for later. As fast as I moved, I stopped just as abruptly, my father's face coming into view. He snarled. My bladder squeezed at the viciousness of the sound and I prayed to whatever deity the Blood Moon brought out that I didn't pee my pants right now. Considering that I was dangling over the doorway to the Underworld, it would be uncouth.

"The time has come," Hades purred. He flicked his wrists, and the ropes lowered me down, though they didn't unwind from around my arms and chest. "We should begin."

I seethed.

Beneath my feet, dark shadows zoomed back and forth, waiting to be set free. I shuddered at the thought of one of those things coming up here. With my body tightly bound, there wasn't much I could do to fight back. All around me, grunts and screams bounced off the walls as witches fought witches. Despite the definite butt kicking my friends brought, the Sisters were stronger. They must have had some sort of protection shield in place because most of the hits barely landed a punch. Not only that, but the circle we so desperately needed to break held strong.

Not to mention their stupid chorus of chants that were starting to give me a migraine. Though that could have been the concussion I was probably milking.

I rubbed the back of my head where I slammed into the wall. "Thanks for the warm welcome," I told Hades.

"We have no time for this," my father replied. His wrists moved again and this time I was dropped down in front of him. The ropes coiled over my ankles to hold me in place like nasty shackles. "Gather!"

Several Sisters left their post and encircled us. While Hades was too busy commanding his blind followers, I scouted the cave. It was hard to make out who was who. I saw a flash of red hair in the distance and the unmistakable largeness of my boyfriend's chest. That and his lime green sweater vest was a dead giveaway. Mom and Joe inched closer toward us, their steps slow and calculated. I noticed the vial of vampire blood in Mom's hand and the glimmer of silver from the knife Joe carried. I needed to buy them time.

"Need a hand?"

My head jerked sideways to Stella. Relief flooded my bones at the sight of my familiar. Stella's brows wiggled as they often did before she followed through with one of her less sane plans. I wanted to tell her to leave before Hades spotted her but it was too late. She was already on the move. Using her ghost energy, she cranked her palms out and shoved one of the Sisters standing behind my father. The woman yelped, stumbling forward clumsily. Unable to stop in time, her shoulder bumped into Hades and he fell forward, knocking into another Sister. It was a chain reaction straight out of a slapstick comedy.

"Zippity zap, Piper," my familiar said. "Use what your daddy gave you!"

I winced. "Stella, gross. Who says—"

My words evaporated. Glaring at my hands that were now entirely covered in blue magic, I widened my stance, understanding dawning on me. I had the same magic as Hades. Well, half of it, which was even better. What if I could combine it with the witch magic I got from Mom?

If this worked, I could be stronger than him. At least I could be in this current state he was in.

Before me, my father's body rippled as he righted himself back to stand. Time was running out. My eyes slipped to the ropes binding me and I did the only thing I could think of. I used my magic on them. Except when I did, I added some creative oomph. My fingers moved fast, and I directed the electrical spark of my magic into the ropes. They let go of my legs instantly, recoiling away and back into the doorway below.

"I don't think so," I said.

Shooting out more of my magic, I swirled my hands, drawing sigils with the electrical current directly over the rift. It hissed and shook, not knowing what to do with the strangeness I was throwing its way. Hovering over the doorway, the black ropes spun in circles, waiting for direction.

One I was willing to provide.

I used every fiber in my body to push the ropes toward Hades. His eyes grew as he understood what was happening, but I had him before he could retaliate. I used the ropes to bind his hands, now knowing it was the core of his magic wielding. Then I dragged him down into his own abyss.

"What are you doing?" my father bellowed.

I smirked. "Time to go home."

One more pull and he would be back where he belonged. I slammed my arm down, a dull pain ripping through me as I was met with resistance. My gaze locked on Hades, who was fighting me tooth and nail. His hands cupped the sides of the rift, refusing to surrender.

"Let go!" I yelled.

"Never!"

My legs started to slide forward from the force. Body coated in sweat, I continued to pump my magic into the ropes to strengthen them, but Hades was too determined to stay.

A gust of wind blew past me as Stella vanished from my side and reappeared next to Hades. "I got this."

"Stella, no!" I screamed.

She didn't listen. The ghost never listened. Giving me a quick wave, my familiar winked and dropped into the rift. My heart jumped into my throat, the pain of losing her overcoming me. What did she do? Why? I had no time to think because, in that same moment, I saw Stella's ghostly arms wrap around Hades and pull him down into the Underworld. She was helping me from within.

My spine uncurled. Footsteps raced toward me. In a moment, I was flanked by my mother and Joe. I glanced at each of them.

"Make it count, honey," Mom breathed out.

And I did.

Using the last of my strength, I pushed out every ounce of magic left in me and slammed it into Hades.

His jaw clicked and a funny expression covered his face. If I had to guess, Hades was both proud and horrified. The ropes shook as they dragged his body back into the Underworld and, as quickly as he appeared, he was gone all the same. The space that my father occupied was empty. He was gone.

Moving rapidly, I rushed to the opening, my eyes searching for Stella. It was so dark, I couldn't make out anything in front of me. Tears flooded my eyes. I blinked them away, continuing the search.

"There!" Joe hollered over my shoulder.

I followed his pointed finger to a pale gray in the midst of all the darkness. It looked an awful lot like fingers. Stella was hanging on. Flattening out on the ground, I cast a quick glance at Joe, then reached in. Whatever power was in the rift shot through me and for the first time in my entire life, I felt invisible. My hand stretched further, and I wrapped my fingers around Stella's arm, pulling her up. Our gazes met as I dragged over the threshold.

Stella turned around, peering into the void she almost drowned in. Her eyes flicked right and left, searching. It was then that I saw she wasn't alone there. Swirling in the black of the rift was another face I'd recognize anywhere.

"Isabella!"

I started to reach for her and Stella joined me, but

the ghost put her palm up to halt us. She shook her head. "I'm good," Isabella said. Looking past us, she found Joe. "You take good care of your girl. Tell your mom Issie misses her."

Oh. So that's how they knew each other. Isabella was friends with Joe's mom. I never would have put the two together. I supposed powerful vamp women were bound to cross paths. Shaking my head to stay on track, I waved at Isabella and stepped aside.

"Thank you," Stella told the other ghost. "For helping me out."

With that, Isabella winked and vanished.

I stood there for a few more minutes, trying to grasp what had happened. A hand pushed me aside as my mother ran past to kneel by the rift. She recited an incantation and opened the vial of vampire blood she held, then dumped it inside. A gasp broke free of me as the rift shut. Gone.

Slowly, I stood on shaky legs, helping Mom up as well. We looked around at the chaos and slumped against each other. Our breaths matched in strained intensity. Around us, the sounds of fighting continued. Everyone was too busy to see that it was over.

My mother wrapped an arm around my shoulder and sighed. "We should probably tell them to stop."

"I'm enjoying the show, actually," Stella said next to me.

Chuckling, I rested my weight against Mom and took in the spectacle. The funny thing was, neither of them was wrong. Was it bad that I kind of enjoyed seeing the witches haul magic at each other, too?

I glanced at the spot where the rift was seconds ago. Perhaps I had more of my father in me than I liked to admit.

CHAPTER 25

Pasta flew in the air at an unexplainable speed. It stuck to the cupboards, the tomato sauce dripping down the white wood and coating it in a mixture a little too close to the color of blood. The smell of garlic and butter wafted up my nose, my mouth twitching.

"Someone get that raccoon out of the kitchen, please," Joe said. His voice was calm, but I could tell he'd had about enough of Harry Houdini trying to steal the food. "Or we'll be eating take out."

"What's wrong with takeout?" Cilia asked.

I crooked a brow her way, grabbing a wet towel to wipe up the mess. "Trust me, Joe's pasta is way better."

Scooping the fusilli into a garbage bin, I cleaned

up the remainder of the sauce and handed Joe a fresh bag of pasta. He got to work immediately, shooting death glares at Harry Houdini, who had already begun running between his legs. As Joe wrestled away the raccoon, I walked to the pantry to get my trusty broom. It was the only thing that could tear Harry away from the food. That and zapping him with magic, but I didn't want to scare the rascal today. I remained convinced he tried to warn me that night. Harry deserved all the pasta his little grubby hands could hold if that was the case.

I lifted the broom and held it up in the air. "Harry!"

The raccoon stopped his attempt at snatching the pan out of Joe's hand to look at me. His little fingers were around the pan's handle, but I saw his resolve weaken.

"If you let Joe finish our meal, I'll give you some of mine." Two fingers unclenched. "And a cookie."

Hissing, the raccoon let go and stalked off, leaving the kitchen and scurrying up the stairs to the second floor. He passed the group of witches lounging on the sofa with zero interest, opting to hide out until I made good on my promise. I completely understood the furball. Why work for your meal when you can have it served to you on a silver platter?

Rolling my eyes, I lowered the broom and rose on

my tiptoes to plant a kiss on Joe's cheek. "Are you sure you don't mind cooking? There's a lot of people here tonight."

My eyes floated past his shoulder to the crowd filling up my home. The evening was Mom's idea and at first, I was reluctant to go through with it. The thought of having Nancy Steeles and her coven over for dinner and drinks was mortifying. It wasn't until Cilia suggested we ask some other people from town over as well that I relaxed. It would be nice to celebrate. After all, the world was still spinning.

Which was exactly how I ended up with a house full of paranormals. Oh, and the sheriff, who was a lot less uncomfortable than I expected. All in all, even with the hitch of the pasta accident, the night was a success.

I raised a glass to my mother, who returned the gesture. She reclined on the sofa, her attention falling back to Nancy, who was animatedly describing an incident that happened at her salon earlier today. I had to hand it to the witch—she could sure tell a story. There would never be a true friendship between me and the coven witches, but this was a start. One I was glad to have agreed to.

After we buried Hades for good, the Sisters of the River disbanded, their life purpose now null and void. Some stayed in the coven to do coffee knows what, while others left, happy to go back to a more simple life. And to come out of the shadows. Mom had mentioned that not everyone in the coven agreed with the head witches, and it was nice to see the truth in her words.

I glanced at the three witches huddled by the fireplace. Nicer even that some of them stayed in Orchard Hollow to help clean up the mess their coven started.

It took four days to seal up the mines with enough magic to deter any further interference. Despite the doorway to the Underworld being sealed, Mom didn't want to take the risk of someone else having the same idea as the Sisters and I deeply agreed. We worked with Nancy's coven and the few Sisters who stayed to get it done. Joe even helped by providing more of his vamp blood for spells. Something I tried not to think about because ew.

After we finished our part, I left it up to Romero to deal with the bureau. They stuck around our little town for two weeks, shoving their noses into everyone's business. Luckily, no one died and the bureau finally packed up their team and left. I'd never seen the sheriff happier than when their black SUVs rolled out of the police lot.

The poor man had enough to deal with in our special town without having eyes on his every move.

A movement by the door caught my eye. I peeled

my gaze from the group in the living room to the front door, watching Stella slip outside. Telling Joe I'll be back in a moment, I followed her out, my chin buried in the thick scarf Mom left on the floor. Now that she announced she was staying, we really needed to discuss cleanliness. One thing my mother was not known for was her organization skills and I could already picture the disaster the farmhouse would become unless I laid down some ground rules. On the plus side, I finally convinced her to stay out of my closet by turning the attic into a large walk-in just for her.

As Gran always said, no one ever said no to a well-calculated bribe.

I stepped out onto the snow covered porch, closing the door behind me with a click. Outside, the driveway was filled with cars and the porch was overflowing with winter boots left by our guests. I had never seen so many people in the farmhouse, not even when Gran was alive. It surprised me how much I enjoyed it.

Finding Stella on the far side of the porch, I padded toward her, resting my palms on the wood railing and following her gaze to the trees on the horizon. "Too rowdy for you in there?" I asked.

The ghost frowned. "Why do you think she did it?"

I didn't have to ask her to clarify; I knew exactly who

Stella meant. Ever since I pulled her out of the rift, her mind has been caught in a loop of thinking about Isabella Beaumont. I tried to talk to Stella about it, but she always shut me down, choosing to wallow in silence instead.

I pulled down the scarf, letting the cold seep into my skin.

"Maybe she knew you had a purpose here," I replied.

"Then why not let you save her too?" Stella asked. "In the end?"

I shrugged, my shoulders staying hiked up for a moment. "I wish I knew," I whispered. "Whatever her reasons were, I'm sure she's happy where she is." Stealing a glance at my familiar, I scooted closer to her. "Joe thinks she found the people she lost there. That she stayed for them."

The ghost stayed silent for a long while. I kept my lips sealed, unwilling to ruin the moment for her. As we stood there with the voice of our friends echoing from the house and the trees dotting the property before us, I couldn't help but smile. We may never know the reasons Isabella had for staying in the Underworld, same as we may never know what Hades planned for our world had he succeeded. What Joe said rang true to the vampire ghost, but I wished to think there was a different reason she stayed behind.

Wherever Isabella was now, I hoped she was giving my father hell.

Next to me, Stella finally pulled her eyes from the woods to look at me. "You should probably go talk to him."

My brow creased.

"Who?" I asked.

Her head nudged past the cars and toward our mailbox at the end of the driveway. Beside it, a man about my age stood quietly, his neck straining to see us on the porch. His body was almost entirely sheer, Joe's truck visible behind him. The man, the ghost, met my gaze and looked away quickly, suddenly finding the snow on the ground very interesting.

I sighed.

"Join me?" I asked Stella.

The ghost gave me a quick nod, then followed behind as I made my way toward the man. When I reached him, his body rippled and vanished, reappearing a second later. As I have learned from Stella in our years of being tethered together, that couldn't be a good sign.

I sucked in a breath, keeping my attention on him. "Hi, there. I'm Piper, this is Stella," I told the ghost. "What's your name?"

"Lance," he answered. "Lance Trovel."

"Good to meet you, Lance. Do you know why you're here?"

The ghost looked up at me, his eyes narrowing. With a quick glance at Stella, he folded his arms over his chest and puffed out his cheeks. "Because I'm dead," he said. "I thought that was a given."

Stella smirked.

"Sure, yes. But why are you at my house?"

"The others said to come," he explained. "They said you could help."

I bit down on my tongue, then rolled it over my front teeth. "Others?"

"Like me," Lance said. His eyes flicked to Stella. "Like us. Ghosts, I suppose. They told me if I needed help to find you. That you'd know what to do."

To say I was confused was an understatement. I always knew that ghosts wouldn't disappear simply because we closed down the rift to the Underworld. Case in point, Stella Rutherford standing beside me. But I didn't realize there were many of them nor that they talked to each other. What I realized even less was that they knew about me.

Clearing my throat, I shoved my hands in the pockets of my coat to keep them warm and asked, "What exactly do you need help with?"

"Finding out who did this to me," Lance replied. "Someone killed me and I need you to find them and make them pay. I was told you're good at this type of thing."

The muscles in my stomach tensed and I had to breathe through the knots forming there. I looked at my familiar, who shot me an encouraging smile but said nothing. This was a lot to take in. Not only were there ghosts out there; now they were sending each other my way like some otherworldly networking system. I could almost laugh.

I didn't, of course. A man was dead.

Turning to look back at the farmhouse, I relaxed my stance and cleared my head. Somehow, I always knew there was no "normal" life for me. But maybe, just maybe, this was what I was meant for.

A clamor sounded from inside the house, followed by Joe and my mother yelling at Harry. I chuckled. Nodding at Stella, I stepped aside and gestured toward the house. "Why don't we go in and talk?"

I watched the two ghosts float to the front door and disappear, my chest warming. One thing was for certain: I would need a lot of coffee to get through this evening. The anticipation of a warm latte hanging before me, I stepped over the threshold and into the house, shutting out the winter wind.

It was good to be home.

LONDON FOG LATTE

Ingredients:
· Earl Grey Tea
· Vanilla extract
· Milk of choice (I like oat for mine)
· Sweetener of choice (I like honey)
· Milk Frother

Instructions:
1. Steep the tea in the same way you normally would to make a cup.
2. Combine vanilla extract, milk, and sweetener in a bowl.
3. Froth the mixture.

4. Pour milk into tea and top off with the froth.

5. Stir and Enjoy!

ABOUT THE AUTHOR

A.N. Sage is a bestselling, award-winning author of mystery and fantasy novels. She has spent most of her life waiting to meet a witch, vampire, or at least get haunted by a ghost. In between failed seances and many questionable outfit choices, she has developed a keen eye for the extra-ordinary.

A.N. spends her free time reading and binge-watching television shows in her pajamas. Currently, she resides in Toronto, Canada with her husband who is not a creature of the night and their daughter who just might be.

A.N. Sage is a Scorpio and a massive advocate of leggings for pants.

For more books and updates:
www.ansage.ca

Connect on social media:
Facebook Group:

facebook.com/groups/945090619339423/

Instagram:

instagram.com/a.n.sage/

TikTok:

tiktok.com/@ansagewrites

YouTube:

youtube.com/c/ANSageWrites

Milton Keynes UK
Ingram Content Group UK Ltd.
UKHW031001020924
447770UK00006B/436